Lucy B. (Lucy Brown) Gregg

Poems in three departments

viz. childhood and youth, religious, and miscellaneous

Lucy B. (Lucy Brown) Gregg

Poems in three departments
viz. childhood and youth, religious, and miscellaneous

ISBN/EAN: 9783337374112

Printed in Europe, USA, Canada, Australia, Japan

Cover: Foto ©Andreas Hilbeck / pixelio.de

More available books at **www.hansebooks.com**

Three Departments,

—viz.—

Childhood and Youth, Religious, and Miscellaneous,

—by—

LUCY B. GREGG.

WM. A. PATTON,

Presbyterian Book Rooms, 7, 8 & 9 Blackford Block,

INDIANAPOLIS.

PREFACE.

LUCY BROWN was born in Sheldon, Vermont, November 7th, 1833; came to Indiana in 1854 to engage as teacher in the Common Schools, returned to Vermont in December, 1855, was married to Charles Gregg, of Carroll county, Indiana, March 18th, 1856. They immediately returned to Indiana and settled on a farm, where they have ever since resided. These poems were written as a recreation while attending to domestic duties, and are put in book form by request of friends, and especially for the gratification of an only son, to whom the work is effectionately dedicated.

CONTENTS.

CHILDHOOD AND YOUTH.

RELIGIOUS.

MISCELLANEOUS.

CHILDHOOD AND YOUTH.

HOBBIES.

It is a trait of human kind
That they to hobbies are inclined;
Seldom, how seldom, one can find
A really even-balanced mind.
    Indeed, I think I never knew
    One altogether so, did you?

I knew a man some years ago,
A person of pretense and show,
Who tried to make his fellows know
They'd better let their hobbies go.
    He said he felt intensely glad
    That he no foolish hobbies had.

He talked this hobby o'er and o'er,
Until we longed to hear no more,
And thought we'd never heard before
Such a disgusting, irksome bore.
    His friends could see that on this point
    His mind was sadly out of joint.

A hobby's really no disgrace,
Though sometimes badly out of place;
It's our plain duty in the case
To treat our friends with patient grace,
    Knowing that likely you and I
    Have hobbies that their spirits try.

ACADEMY DAYS.

I don't forget, I can't forget,
    I would not if I could;
"Twould seem to me like sacrilege,
    Or folly if I should.
The good old ways of otner days,
    The days of ripening youth;
When in the old Academy,
    We conned the works of truth.

Those lessons good, well understood,
    Will never be forgot;
The lively emulation there,
    Will positively not.
I'll not forget, in my own case,
    How well I understood;
Parental care, had placed me there,
    For my especial good;

Though time and means were limited;
  If I but did my best,
God, in his kindly providence,
  Would manage all the rest.

I've not forgot the well built house,
  Its high clean white-washed walls,
Its ample recitation rooms,
  Its well swept stairs and halls;
The merry bell, that used to tell,
  Us when and where to go,
While we so gay, glad to obey,
  Went tramping to and fro.

I'll ne'er forget the principal,
  His counsel good and wise,
Nor his assisting fair young spouse,
  With kindness in her eyes;
Nor, the grave advanced assistant,
  Who strutted with a cane;
And seemed as much above us all,
  As rooster on a vane.
His words of spice meant for advice,
  Came down on every one;
Nor would he bear an idle stare,
  Or injudicious fun.

I can't forget my classmates good,
   Those jolly girls and boys;
Young gentlemen and ladies fine,
   Despite a little noise.
The exercise witty and wise,
   On Friday afternoon,
By one required to take a part,
   Is not forgotten soon.

On Tuesday night with great delight,
   The literary met;
School-girl might go with school-boy beau,
   I recommend it yet,
But on the greatest day of all,
   Examination day;
Class after class the test would pass,
   With more or less display.
Then comes the fervent fond good-bye,
   Hushed now is youthful mirth;
Parting we go, but who can know,
   If meeting comes on earth?

A TEASING BROTHER.

A great way off and long ago.
I woke near mountains topped with snow,

Grew just as other babies grow,
Learned what such rustic maidens know.

I had a brother, and think he
Meant always to be kind to me;
But being senior years by three,
He did delight in teasing me.

He was a handsome gifted boy,
Was all my pride, had been my joy,
But, oh how much he could annoy
His little sister, playmate, toy!

He told with an open heart,
And with an accent rather tart,
That in whate'er I took a part,
I showed I was not very smart.

I was too pert, he wisely said,
And held too high my ugly head;
I'd better far be sent to bed,
And on some baby pudding fed.

He could not think what I did mean.
By always trying to be seen;
He would inform me I was green,
A dowdy, dumpy " Daisy Dean."

And this continued till I own.
Before I was a woman grown
Much of my love for him had flown;
I wanted to be let alone.

But still he teased me day by day,
Until I knew not what to say,
And almost wished to get away—
He made it irksome there to stay.

At length there came a way for me
To slip out easy as could be;
Of course a girl so young and free
Would like this wondrous world to see.

An older brother far away
A flying visit came to pay,
And in a week—almost a day—
He bore me with him far away.

A trip they said would soon be o'er,
Then I'd be with them as before;
But ah, that going proved far more.
Those tiresome teasing days were o'er !

I ne'er returned with them to stay,
Was there when mother passed away,

And there observed my nuptial day,
But home's a thousand miles away.

A score of years and more have flown,
And bub and I have wiser grown,
Yet each has in a quiet home
But little of the other known.

And when we reach the shining shore,
Where human foibles all are o'er,
I'll not be foolish as before,
Nor will he tease me any more.

A TEASING SISTER.

I am a doting brother bold,
And one that does not like to scold;
I have a merry sister bright,
Who ought to be my home delight.
    Our little Nell is quite a belle,
But, being saucy as can be,
She will not take advice from me.

She thinks I ought to tell her now
The why, the wherefore, and the how,
Of all I've studied out or read,

And what the latest speaker said,
　She wants to know just where I go,
Exactly what I do while there,
Precisely what the ladies wear.

This little tiresome teasing elf
Is five years younger than myself,
And since I'm willing to protect,
I feel entitled her respect,
　And may have, though, I do not know,
She's most too much of childish glee
To be quite understood by me.

She says that like a dolt I look,
Forever poring o'er a book;
I'm growing selfish, cold and proud,
Why can't I sometimes read aloud?
　A placid smile, once in a while.
Would so become my manly face,
She thinks a laugh is no disgrace.

My dear old aunt, Jerusha Ann,
Thinks I will make a noble man;
And then she gives a sigh for Nell,
And says, indeed I can not tell,
　She is too pert, a dreadful flirt,

One of the wildest girls in town,
Oh, how she needs to steady down.

Still father says the child means right,
Though such a careless, erring sprite;
To mother adds (with roguish wink)
I knew another once, I think.
    He is to bad, it makes me sad—
But mother's such a loving saint,
She bears the joke without complaint.

Sometimes I thing perhaps she knows
More on the subject than she shows,
And that the girls in other days
Had jolly, wayward winning ways.
    And that is why they do not try
To stop at once this tiring tease,
But bear her pranks with gracious ease.

EGOTISM.

We all are egotistical,
    In one way or another;
Still, few things do we more dislike,
    In sister friend or brother.

There's mother B—, she's kind to thee,
  But then its I so often;
You can but fear, her time is near,
  When brain not heart will soften.

Brisk thrifty G—, it's plain to see,
  Is useful in his way;
Yet that shrewd man's an egotist;
  And has to much to say,
Of what he's done, and what begun,
  Which, when it is completed,
Will show the world his purposes
  Are not to be defeated.

Sweet singer E—, from harshness free,
  In solo soft or loud;
It's understood, would do more good,
  If she were not so proud.
Young brother A—, can talk and pray,
  In unknown tongue and high,
But that seems egotistical;
  And doth not edify.

Good pastor Tall above us all,
  In theologic lore
Were he less large could help his charge,

And serve his master more,
And you and I, when'er we try
To show off some perfection;
Are sure to show (what others know),
We're vain in that direction.

PUT YOURSELF IN MY PLACE.

Before you credit much that comes
    Through gossip and her clan,
Think of the harm that they have done
    To woman and to man ;

Think when sad truth was bad enough,
    How falsehood made it worse ;
Think of the good that might have been
    But for this blighting curse.

And ere you chide me for my fault
    Or brand me with disgrace,
Be sure justice demands assault :
    Put yourself in my place.

And if you find I have done wrong,
    O'ercome in trial's hour,
Be honest; are you always strong
    Above the tempter's power?

Remember, those who dwell in frail,
  Brash houses made of glass,
May come to trouble if they throw
  At others as they pass.

Be guided by the word of God,
  Let it decide the case;
That is the only way you can
  Put yourself in my place.

NO RULES FOR COURTIN.

There's rules for makin bread and cheese
  And there is rules for eatin;
There's rules for every thing you please,
  Both while to home or meetin;
But there's no rules and cannot be
  For this, the best of sportin;
Jest 'cause the parti's all agree
  They'll have no rules for courtin.

We know that sittin on the stile
  Sounds dreffle nice in rhymin,
And hangin on a gate awhile
  Jest beats the moon a shinin.

Some think while sailin on a lake,
Or ridin on a river,
Is jest the nicest time to take
To captivate a lover.

The old folks like to stay to home,
Say that's the place for talkin,
But girls and boys would rather roam
And simper sweets a walkin.
Oh how they love to buggy ride,
Jest as the sun is settin;
They 'magine sittin side by side
There'll never be no frettin.

In vain we tell sich folks to stop—
Where one goes t'other'll foller,
Let it be to the mountain top
Or to the shady holler.
But still I doubt if times would be
One mite or grain the better
If courtin was controlled by me
And had rules to the letter.

WAS COURTIN.

Our schoolhouse was a beauty,
All painted red and white;

And there was meetin' to it,
    Most every Sunday night.

Poor, dear old Parson Commonplace
    Was troubled with catarrh;
No words rolled smoothly from his face,
    But came with kinder jar.

So, 'course, we young folks didn't go
    Jest 'zactly for the preachin';
But took for granted all was so,
    Whatever he was teachin'.

But oh! the singin' it was nice,
    When Zekel Jones he started;
It 'minded one of kind advice
    Gi'n to the chicken-hearted.

I allus tried to do my best
    To make the treble sweeter;
But Sally Brown beat all the rest
    In any kinder meter.

'Twas jest as plain as A B C
    Who loved the charmin' critter;
And that her name would soon be Smith,
    If John could only git her.

But somehow 'twas not quite so plain
  Who 'Zekel was admirin';
He seemed so kinder distant like,
  So bashful and retirin.'

One awful cold and shiny night,
  I never can forgit it;
The moon could not have shone more bright
  If Cupid's breath had lit it.

My heart stood still as any stump,
  Then went off in a flutter,
When 'Zekel driv up to our door
  In his new painted cutter.

Of course I went; why shouldn't I?
  With fur robes tucked around me;
And if there'd been lots more of cold,
  I 'spect it couldn't found me.

I'll never tell jist what we said,
  It mayn't be worth reportin';
But from that blessed night I knew
  Who 'Zekel Jones was courtin'.

EVIL SPEAKING.

I knew an old woman not very tall,
Indeed the poor dame was exceedingly small,
But there was one thing unpleasant to find,
Her body was quite as large as her mind.

She'd short bushy hair, cheek sallow and thin,
A leaden blue eye, with peak nose and chin,
No grace or beauty, from coarse shoe to crown,
A fussy old maid, in a faded old gown.

Father or mother she never had known;
Brother or sister she'd not of her own;
She clung to cousins, a burdensome charge,
In poverty's home of family large.

She could spin and knit, that was about all,
With needle awkward, for heavy work small,
Though simple, yet comic, talky and queer,
Visiting seemed her appropriate sphere.

For ten miles around her calling was known,
And pitiful kindness to her was shown;
About once a year her circuit she made,
A day and a night was as long as she stayed.

Now when I was little, I wondered much,
Why mother carefully entertained such;

And when she noticed it puzzled my brain,
Then she consented the cause to explain.

She said Vina's foolish, tiresome and flat,
Not entertaining one bit in her chat;
But she is harmless, as harmless can be,
And never speaks evil of others to me.

My pliable mind the matter took in;
Ma thought evil speaking terrible sin,
I'd nothing to say; it taught me more good
Than any amount of lecturing could.

Though not very smart, this story is true;
It has a moral more lasting than new;
Oft when I'm tempted to speak rather free,
Conscience says "never speaks evil to me."

THEY SAY.

Please do not tell me what they say;
  I've no desire to know;
I'd rather hear what Peggy says.
  Tom, Dick, Harry or Joe.

3

For when one knows the author's name
   He has a chance to judge;
How much of all he hears is true,
   And how much false and fudge.

But they say's too indefinite,
   It may be true or not;
And often even they say truths
   Had better be forgot.

WICKED LITTLE AZARO.

Far, far from mother, love and joy,
Poor Azaro was a homesick boy;
With no wise father's counsel blest,
No brother's presence cheered his rest,
From tender sister torn away,
With maiden aunts compelled to stay;
None seemed to understand his case,
Nor why the child disliked his place.
And so he drifted day by day,
Far from the straight and narrow way;
Became a hard and wicked lad,
And every body called him bad.

He had no very fixed belief,
His thoughts on sacred things were brief;
He'd heard there was a God of love,
If so, he must be far above
The world with which he had to do:
None loved him where he was, he knew.
Likewise he'd heard of heaven and hell,
But he was young; and very well;
They too, like God, were far away,
He'd think, of them some other day,
Sad, sad the state of this bad boy.
Far, far from mother, love and joy.

His aunts saw little need of play,
Thought precious time was thrown away;
Meant to restrain him while they could,
Then wondered why he was not good.
Defiance marred his fair young face,
Rebellion plunged him in disgrace;
He grew familiar with the rod,
More so than with the word of God;
And though by far more knave than fool,
He showed no taste for books or school,
He only showed a love of play,
And for it often ran away.

Oh, what a dreadful wicked boy!
Far, far from mother, love and joy.

He went on errands far and near,
In every season of the year,
And this he liked, for when away
He always took a snatch of play,
Which he denied both loud and strong.
When told that he had stayed too long.
One very cold and windy day,
Astride of horse he rode away;
He tried to whistle and be brave,
But still the heartless wind would shave;
His pants were short, his coat was thin,
He ne'er before so cold had been.
One mile, two miles, a half mile more,
Before he reached the neighbor's door,
He gave one loud, imploring rap,
Then marched straight in and doffed his **cap,**
The mistress seemed to be alone,
Spoke in a kind and friendly tone;
This fair young cherished christian bride
Feigned not to notice that he cried,
But talked away with quiet cheer;
Said it is cold to-day my dear,

You've had a disagreeable ride,
Accept a cake that I have fried.
The boy was touched, his heart was won,
A better life was then begun;
He thought, and thought, and thought again
Thought both of women and of men,
Thought how he'd like that home to share,
A home so full of loving care,
What thoughts for such a wicked boy!
Far, far from mother, love and joy.

Next day he said in childish way,
I'd like to live with Mr. J——.
His friends replied, perhaps you can,
You there might learn to be a man;
We've little for a boy to do,
A farm would be the place for you,
Did he hear right, and was it so,
Would they be willing he should go?
What joy, what hope, what glad surprise!
New light seemed beaming from the skies!

The farmer and his gentle wife,
Removed from city's whirl and strife,
Though notified that he was bad,
Concluded they would try the lad.

They each possessed a cultured mind,
Commenced with him both firm and kind,
And it's a truth worthy to tell,
He always pleased them very well;
Soon learned to work as well as play,
Nor did he from them run away;
Was both obedient and spry,
And never once told them a lie.
Great the reform in this bad boy,
Far, far from mother, love and joy.

Fifty eventful years have flown,
The boy a gray-haired man has grown,
He's led a humble life of prayer,
Filled tutor's and professor's chair;
A firm believer of the truth,
He proves a guide to halting youth.
This faithful servant of the Lord
From sacred desk proclaims his word;
Lives in a peaceful, quiet home,
With no desire to change or roam,
He has a daughter, only one,
And God hath given him no son;
That daughter dwells in heathen land,
One of a missionary band,

And there she toils year after year,
With faith that makes her duty clear.
Her father, with parental care,
Is constant in prevailing prayer,
That God will shield her by his might,
His presence make her burden light,
And when she lays her armor down,
Saved heathen souls may deck her crown.
Strange prayer for one who when a lad,
Was known to be extremely bad,
But time and grace have changed the boy,
Far, far from mother, love and joy.

A HEN.

I think a hen's a funny *critter*,
She's always scratching in a litter;
And if the litter's full of dirt
She gives it such a happy flirt.

The little chickens all are chicks,
And any hen can hover six;
But one that gives an extra squat
Can cover twelve as well as not.

A hen that is superbly fed,
One of wlde wings, and wiser head,
A tip-top extra superfine,
Can hover two or three times nine.

My friend possessed a speckled pet,
I never knew her equal yet—
She strutted round with thirty-eight,
And raised them all and kept them straight.

A KIND WORD.

A kind word, though often heard,
  We wish to hear it more;
It does us good, it always would,
  If multiplied threescore.

To souls in grief it brings relief;
  It cheers the lonely heart;
To stricken saint, weary and faint,
  It comfort doth impart.

The erring one, almost undone,
  It even doth reclaim;
He tries again, like wiser men,
  To earn an honest name.

Such words are cheap, why should we speak,
    If we must speak unkind;
We'd better be from harsh words free,
    And of a gentle mind.

SCHOOL THIRTY YEARS AGO.

WRITTEN, 1880.

In grand New England, land of hills, just thirty years
    ago,
I taught school at Corners, and waded through the
    snow;
My thoughts go back in thankful mode to those
    eventful days,
Of happy, busy, sturdy thrift and Puritanic ways.
Poor, frail, shy girl, of eighteen years, in this wide
    world of strife,
With father's blessing, mother's prayers, I started out
    in life.
How very broad the world appeared; how much I
    found to learn
Of solid truth, fit to impart to others in their turn.

The Corners was a grand old place; nature had made
  it so;

Green Mountains met the rising sun; white valleys
  smiled below.

The hills, those everlasting hills, what giveth more
  delight,

Than native, solid, rocky hills, bedecked in green and
  white?

The school house, little bee-hive thing, was crowded
  to the fill;

Appeared like mammoth birdsnest, stuck in crevice of
  the hill.

Sometimes I almost thought I was the woman in the
  shoe,

Who had so many children that she knew not what
  to do.

But how I loved that jolly throng, from chubby
  A, B, C,

To sturdy Jonathan who strove with double rule of
  three;

Bright little girls in pantalets, from five to eight or
  nine,

To Miss who'd been one term away, and wrote un-
  common fine.

Of course the grade was rather mixed, extending all
the way
From a-b ab, and o-x ox, to Davies' Algebra.
But they were quite obedient, and tried to do their
best;
While I so young, was hopeful, too, and happy with
the rest;
All muffled up, and well prepared for stormy winds
that blow,
We thought but little more of cold than doth the
Esquimaux.
Nature imparted hardihood, and snow-bird like
we'd go,
With nimble feet mid ice and sleet o'er crusted banks
of snow.
Some people think that boarding 'round is not so very
nice;
But I received the best of fare, and plenty of advice:
A poor dejected invalid gave me the rules of health,
Another person (very poor) marked out the road to
wealth,
And one whom I had cause to fear was not uncom-
mon good,
Seemed very sure that she the way to Heaven under-
stood.

My parents, long before, had taught that it was rude
    of me,
When seniors gave me their advice, to seem to disagree.
So when I simply bowed assent, replied I understood,
They each esteemed me wise enough to do their chil-
    dren good.
Thanksgiving there meant "lots of fun"—you've
    heard of that before,
And merry Christmas came around as in the days of
    yore;
The fathers, with great double sleighs, gave all an
    invitation,
On Christmas eve, to ride with them to the illumina-
    tion.
The church, adorned, was beautiful, the service
    praise and prayer,
But Santa Claus, I know not why, was not admitted
    there.
Neither were presents thrown around, as in these lat-
    ter days,
But still my heart doth ever long for those old-fash-
    ioned ways.
Much has been said, and wrote, and sung, of mothers
    everywhere;
But, fathers, kind, indulgent souls—God bless the
    fathers there.

SABBATH SCHOOL FORTY YEARS AGO.

WRITTEN, 1884.

Precious, joyous memories are treasured in my brain;
My spirit sings a grateful song, my heart a glad refrain,

When I think of our old school-house, both pine without and in;
Which stood unfenced beside the road, and ne'er had
painted been.

High, grand Green mountains framed the east, and
Champlain's vale the west;
While hillside beauties were increased by streams in
glad unrest.

'Twas there were taught the rudiments of science and
of art.;
For writing then, and drawing too, of learning was a
part.

But, in these fast, progressive days, who makes the
greatest scrawl
Is thought to be the most advanced, and smartest one
of all.

And there we met for Sabbath-school; no kind of
  bell to chime;
We learned to do like wiser souls, watch and redeem
  the time.

No organ, and no lesson leaf; we still, with faces
  bright,
Went gladly to the Sabbath-school, our verses to
  recite.

"In the beginning was the Word;" and then "The
  Word was light."
These and like texts and contexts were repeated with
  delight.

Doubtless we did not understand like some great
  learned divine;
This much I knew, it cheered and blessed the little
  heart of mine.

What if their were no papers crisp, and colored cards
  around;
King James' version of the word, was full of doctrine
  sound.

Some truths need never be explained; we often err, I
  fear,
In trying to make axioms more potent, plain and
  clear.

Our library of English works, though second-hand at
    best,
Contained some choice biographies, and tales to
    interest.

They treated much of peasant life, so all unlike our
    own;
Facts, well worth knowing, but for those we never
    might have known.

Our teachers had our confidence; we loved to hear
    them pray;
To join with them in Zion's songs, in good old fash-
    ioned way.

If there be now a better mode, we then knew naught
    about it,
And, in our blissful ignorance, accepted life without
    it.

Time's searching winds of forty years have blown
    the chaff away;
While good fruits of that Sabbath-school remain unto
    this day.

Our teachers all have reached the home where many
    mansions are;
And, if we'er faithful to our Lord, we soon shall en-
    ter there.

MEDDLESOME.

A vain old turkey went to walk,
In quiet grandeur did she stalk;
She held her head extremely high,
Observing both the fields and sky.
At length she spied, beside a wall,
A something shapely as a ball;
She said "How careless some will be,
I'll show what can be done by me.
That egg needs care without a doubt;
I'll sit on it and hatch it out."
Two seconds only did it take
To hatch it out, all wide awake,
For 'twas a hornets nest you see,
And in a dreadful plight was she!
How that wise hen did hop about,
Her bill went bobbing in and out;
Humiliation fear and pain,
Gave her poor nerves an awful strain.

———

The moral of this tale is clear;
With other homes don't interfere;
Some humble homes of no pretense
Have telling means of self-defense.

UNCOMMON WISE.

I'm sorry for the common man,
  So meagerly he's taught;
It's not expected that he can
  Possess much depth of thought.
But I, who have been through college,
  And schools of science too;
Shall expect you to acknowledge
  I'm in advance of you.

And since I have been across the seas,
  Seen towers and steeples tall;
My thoughts have such unbounded scope,
  I'm sure I know it all.
Not only wise but doubly so,
  I've knowledge overflowing,
And if there's aught I do not know,
  That little's not worth knowing.

A SUMMER SHOWER.

Hurlyburly, fluster, flout;
What is all this stir about?
Hoity, toity, flurry fly;
Clouds go whirling through the sky.

Whistling o'er the hill, the gale
Whizzes through the sultry vale.
Exit now oppressive warm,
Swallowed by the coming storm.

Vivid zigzag lightnings flash ;
Thunders roll with direful crash ;
Rain comes pouring with a dash,
Through the shutters, down the sash,
Giving all a wholesome plash.
Scented vines the casement thrash,
'Till they fall a beaten mash,
Worse than Bridget's morning hash.
As they back and forward lash ;
Signs and awnings go to smash,
Strewing sidewalks with their brash,
Paltry, torn and broken trash.
Dandy with his gay calash,
Treated to unwelcome splash,
Quite crestfallen and abash,
Thinks the visit rather rash.

Rather rash, but blest the hour
When the sky begins to lower.
Nature manifests her power
In the purifying shower.

Invalid, relieved of pain;
Farmer, thoughful of his grain ;
Captain School-boy and his train ;
All send up the glad refrain :
"Small the loss, and great the gain,
Coming with the needed rain."

PLAYING TOO BIG.

Once on a time, as stories say,
Two jolly brothers went to play;
One boy was five, the other ten,
And both were noble little men.
They played contented on the green,
Till Jimmy Sharpe, about thirteen,
Came round with his new bat and ball,
And stopped to make a friendly call.
This threw Sir Five-years in the shade;
Yet no complaint by him was made;
He only slipped back to the house
As quiet as a little mouse,
Crept in behind the kitchen door,
As he had done when grieved before;
And there he sobbed his sorrow out
Until his mother came about

And said: Why Sammy! are you here?
You ought to play with Lewis, dear!
He heard her with a lengthened face
Like culprit in a graver case,
Then gave his moistened eyes a dig,
And whimpered, "Lewis plays too big!"

Proud, stately dames of good intent,
Willing to spend and to be spent,
Are loth to own or understand
When they are playing over-grand.

Learned editors, both grave and wise,
Are led to taunt and criticise;
And this they do with the pretense
Of acting in but self-defense.
Their patrons in the vale below,
Don't comprehend or try to know
Why each should on the other charge:
We only know they're playing large.

The man of God, gifted and blest,
Has grace enough to stand the test
He passes through in daily life,
In this unfriendly world of strife;
Yet, when he preaches, off he'll fly :
Playing too big—shooting too high.

Even the teachers of our youth,
Whose words may all be solid truth,
By haughty look, sarcastic thrust,
Fill precious hopeful with disgust;
He cannot love, he may not hate
His teachers while they're playing great.

Thus do the great, the good of earth,
People of wisdom, wit and worth;
Those who in mines of knowledge dig,
Err sadly by their playing big.

A LITTLE BOY'S MISSIONARY SPEECH.

"You'd scarce expect one of my age,
Who never spoke upon the stage,
To make a very pretty show,
Or tell you much you do not know.
I only know the earth is round,
And people everywhere are found,
That God is good, and men are bad,
And I'm a silly little lad.
I've heard the chief great end of man,
Is serving God the best he can,

And that is more than some have heard,
Poor heathen do not know a word
About the Father and the Son,
And God the spirit, three in one,
Nor of the great salvation plan
That offers pardon unto man.
And that is why we come and say
Please take our pennies, that they may
Be ready for those folks to use
Who go to tell the blessed news.
I've only seen one missionary
That was our own dear, sweet Miss Carey.
She looked exactly like a girl;
   Had she been my big sister
I should not have been one bit afraid
   To have stepped right up and kissed her."

THIS WICKED WORLD AND I.

This wicked world will not do right;
   And I have thought of late,
That if I try, until I die,
   I cannot keep it straight.

I have a clear exalted view
  Of what the world should be;
But it's too fast, I've found at last,
  To be controlled by me.

Some think the world is better now
  Than in the days of yore,
But if it's so I fail to know
  How bad it was before;
For now it's full of deadly strife,
  Of vanity and show,
Of idle din and direful sin,
  That ends in human woe.

I live in Consequential town,
  On Egotistic street,
I'm wondrous wise in my own eyes,
  My name is Self-Conceit;
I've told the world just what I think,
  But it don't seem to hear;
If it goes down, like Sodom town,
  My conscience will be clear.

GIRLS' WRONGS.

I read not long ago about
  The rights and wrongs of boys,
And how they never have a chance
  To make enough of noise.

If those same boys were in my place
  On music-lesson day,
And had to make a noise by rule,
  I wonder what they'd say

I've very little fault to find
  With common jolly boys;
Their games are really extra fine,
  And I admire their noise.

But they are very ignorant
  If they don't understand
That girls have wrongs as well as boys,
  And snubs on every hand.

I do not mean sweet little girls,
  Just big enough to pet,
But awkard, romping girls like me,
  Not quite young ladies yet.

I tried to run about with boys
  A little once or twice;

But soon I found my brothers thought
   That was not very nice.

They said they'd like my company
   If 'twasent for the looks;
But girls were made to play with dolls
   And look at picture books.

Now that was such a dreadful snub,
   I took a lengthy pout,
And acted like a naughty girl
   I've not the slightest doubt.

Whene'er I try to do my best,
   I show my greenness worse;
And Aunt Jerusha Ann's remarks
   Are more acute and terse.

So when accomplished people call
   With all their polished airs,
I beat a shy but sure retreat
   Upon the garret stairs.

I've always heard that going down
   Afforded poor relief;
And so I try by going up
   To soar above my grief.

There I can hear the boys without,
   Piping their merry songs;
Oh, how I long to be with them,
   With them forget my wrongs.

LOOKING OUT, AND LOOKING IN.

I saw the portraits of two men,
It doth not matter where nor when;
They were alike in age and size,
But quite unlike all otherwise,
One with great, daring wicked eyes,
A tiger seemed in poor disguise,
He was forever looking out
To see what others were about;
But felt afraid to look within,
He had a heart so full of sin.
A pistol lay at his right hand,
To give the world to undestand
He held himself in a condition
That would admit no opposition.
An infidel of direst dye;
Who e'en his Maker did deny;

With heart that knew no godly fear,
Nor held its fellow-being dear.
All this I saw in portrait first;
A mortal by his deeds accursed,
Vain sophist, plunged in dread and doubt,
In worldly wisdom "looking out."

The other portrait, soiled and quaint,
Was of an aged, confiding saint,
Who, by God's help had conquered sin,
Until he loved to look within.
God's book before him open wide,
No pistol needed at his side;
He looked (with his spectacles on)
As though he might be reading John,
Or else his righteous soul, may be,
Was feasting on Psalm Twenty-three;
A servant working for the right,
A Christian walking in the light,
Whose path grew brighter day by day,
The more he learned to watch and pray;
At peace with God and all mankind,
And schooled to bear the woes we find,
Long years of usefulness were passed,
He'd almost reached the goal at last.

Within he felt his sins forgiven,
A sure and steadfast hope of heaven.
How sweet, 'mid earthly toil and din,
To be thus soothed by "looking in."

LOVE.

Since poets great, and rhymers small,
  Makes love a blind affair;
Conscience demands, I make it plain,
  With thoughts I have to spare.

Claiming to know far more of love,
  Than those who flaunt or flout it;
I really do believe, I know
  All need be known about it.

I've loved for over fifty years
  Of woman's checkered life;
Loved in the balmy days of peace,
  And through our Nation's strife.

Yet all the harm I've seen of love,
  Resulted from the twitter
Of some poor foolish girl or boy,
  With a deceiving critter.

I tell the truth, though love is queer,
   With contracts strange and striking;
You'll find it nothing more nor less,
   Than a tremendous liking.

WE BOYS.

The world has come to such a pass,
We boys are an afflicted class;
Men, women, girls, do all conspire
To thwart us when we but desire
To make a joyous hearty noise;
Which is the honest right of boys.

We boys are sharp enough to see
That girls have better times than we;
The girls can ride, we boys must walk;
We boys must listen, while they talk;
We boys must push, if girls would swing;
But may not whistle while they sing.

Sometimes I think we're hardly needed;
By girls we are so superseded;
But then we're good for folks to scold,
To stand the heat and brave the cold,
To run on errands when desired,
And never cheep if we are tired.

While others sit, we boys must stand;
Ready to move at their command;
We're simply servants any way;
Servants without the servant's pay—
We boys think strange men have forgot
The trials of the urchin's lot.

But wait, we boys shall soon be men;
We shall be kind of sovereigns then;
We'll make and execute the laws,
Enforcing this benignant clause;
We do decree that all the boys
Shall be allowed to make a noise.

GREEN BOYS

Of all the men I ever knew,
The gifted were a precious few;
And of those few the best I've seen
Were in their youth accounted green.

The great divines of whom I've read,
Both living and the honored dead,
When boys, were closely cooped at night,
Learning to read and spell and write.

In early years, and years of late,
The pilots of the ship of State,
While young were happy as a king
If tied to mother's apron string.

I cannot think what people mean
By caring if their boys are green;
The law allows each mother's son
To be a boy—till twenty-one.

And if still green at twenty-three,
It's just as well; for, don't you see,
Some of the wisest men alive
Were noted green at twenty-five.

A boy's fresh, laughing, honest face
Is quite reviving in its place;
Reserve for men the polished mein—
I wish that all the boys were green.

IRISH MOTHER'S ADVICE.

Oh, Larrey, me honey list thou to thy mither,
Ye've had only one, and ye'll ne'er have anither,
So Larrey, me darling, be asy, me man,
And if ye canna be asy, be asasy's ye can.

If the craps do be light, and the rents do be high,
Would it make matters better to sit down and cry?
Nay, niver me darling—work aisy, me man;
And if ye canna be aisy, be as asy's ye can.

Should Nora and Bridget both give ye up,
Do never go moping, or take to the cup,
There's good baef in market as iver was bought—
Good fish in the sae as iver was caught;
So, Larrey, me darling, be asy me man,
And if ye canna be asy, be as asy's ye can.

Whativer betide ye, howe'er bad yer luck,
Don't drive yerself crazy by loosing yer pluck;
The darkest of night is succaded by day,
The greatest of troubles will soon pass away,
So, Larrey, me darling, be asy, me man,
And if ye canna be asy, be as asy's ye can.

THE SLEIGH-RIDE.

'Tis evening's hour, the sky is clear,
And laughing do the stars appear,
The moon walks forth with visage bright,
To crown the glory of the night.

Upon a night so apt for play,
When books and slates are laid away,
What music in the sleigh-bell's sound,
When first we hear them coming round.

Hurrah! now mother, may I go?
, Here is my shawl—now don't say no,
For they have stopped before the door,
One, three, five, seven, ten or more!

How swiftly are we borne away,
With cheerful looks and laughter gay,
And ere we think it can be so,
We have no further now to go!

As we return, oh! do, I pray,
Let us go round a longer way!
Say! are you cold? I'm sure I'm not,
Although my mittens I've forgot.

But really! we are almost home!
How swiftly they will think we've come;
Indeed, I think we almost fly—
And here we are! so now, good-bye!

MISFORTUNES NOT FAULTS.

Misfortunes are not faults they say,
But the results of nature's sway.
We all are governed by her power,
And subject to them every hour.

Yet it's a truth extremely sad,
The worst misfortunes that I've had,
Were the results of indiscretion,
Or lurking faults in my prossession.

Misfortunes are not faults we're told.
Yet "I was young and now I'm old,"
The righteous I've not seen forsaken,
Nor yet their seed by want o'ertaken.

Afflictions come unto the good,
Our Father orders that they should,
But he who meekly bears the rod,
Has proof that he's a child of God.

Faults are misfortunes, that we know,
The direct cause of grief and woe,
But trials that in faults don't rise,
I think "are blessings in disguise."

DIFFERENT THINKS.

A four year old quite full of glee,
Was by his mother left with me,
Just through the middle of the day,
While she a list of calls could pay.

He with his questions sounded me.
And in most things we could agree.
But he at length, a subject found
On which he thought I was not sound.

But his Lordship would not combat,
He was much too polite for that,
At length he said with knowing winks
" People must have different thinks,"

The foolish girl of seventeen
Thinks she's as graceful as a queen,
She's often vexed at her mama,
And dreadful shamed of poor papa.

A sire and dame have brows bent low,
And oft escapes a sigh of woe,
Lest her they love should find at last
The life she's led has been too fast,

And then we have another case.
Where children try to know their place,

And parents are so hard to please
A child is never at its ease.

We meet such cases on our way,
Indeed we see them every day,
And oft my heart within me sinks
Cause people have such different thinks.

We know prim Aramantha Bliss,
Who greets each sister with a kiss—
Just aggravates aunt Polly Stout
Who knows so well what she's about.

Aud when Philucia Butterfly
Hopes she's a mansion in the sky,
Behold how Tommy Comic blinks—
He knows what Mrs. Wordling thinks.

Old Deacon Cheery of our town,
Who in his youth was quite a clown,
In many things can't see the harm,
When Elder Graves sounds the alarm.

These men are both possessed of grace,
And each is useful in his place.
No doubt their chains of life have links
Which have produced their "different thinks."

Happy the one whose soul refined,
To evil thoughts is not inclined,
And whose whole heart and spirit shrinks
From chiding others for their "thinks."

SMALL BOY'S OPINION OF GRAND-FATHERS.

Grandfathers are the best of folks;
　That's my profound belief.
They tell a fellow fine old jokes,
　And help him out of grief.

They aid him through the hardest work,
　Then let him help them rest;
And never make him use his fork
　Where knives are lots the best.

They let you ride with them to mill,
　When it's a pleasant day;
And don't say "hush" "and do be still,"
　At every thing you say.

In winter time they mend the skates,
　And carts in summer time;
Nor chide a boy for likes and hates,
　That may not be sublime.

Grandfather proves an advocate
  With father and with mother;
And who like him can palliate
  A big exacting brother.

I do not know what I should do—
  How sad my life would be—
Without a dear Grandpa or two,
  What would become of me?

MOTHER'S IMPERFECTION.

The boy at first thinks mother is
  An object of perfection,
And that her conduct calleth not
  For comment or inspection.
His first ten years she soothes and cheers;
  And gives him fond protection.
If wise and good, its understood,
  Is just in her correction.

But during youth he finds in truth,
  That like himself she's human;
Imagines he great faults can see;
  Since she is but a woman.

Then ten to one the mother's son
  Starts off on the wrong track;
Soon shows that he can saucy be,
  And doth discretion lack.

When older grown, his wild oats sown,
  If given to reflection,
Thoughts of these days of wayward ways
  Are sad in retrospection.

When mother's dead, pert words he said
  Return in recollection;
He finds too late, his loss is great,
  Though she was not perfection.

MINISTER'S SON.

Oh, wonder of wonders, and wonder outdone—
The best boy in town is the minister's son!
Nor is he the person to tell you about it,
Displaying his goodness lest somebody doubt it.

He asks and receiveth attention but small;
We give our approval by silence—that's all;
But if he were forward, mischievous and bad,
Then all the good people would notice the lad.

Oh, wonder of wonders!—and yet I'm inclined
To think many cases there be of the kind;
And that the poor scape-goat—the minister's son—
Is charged with much evil he never hath done.

JOHN SMITH'S COMPLAINT.

I am an honest citizen,
   As any man in town,
I'm just as good as Peter Jones,
   Or Ebenezer Brown.

I try to mind my business,
   Like any man of sense;
And take care of the dollars,
   By caring for the pence.

I always have been temperate,
   And paid my honest dues.
So never have occasion,
   To mind my P's and Q's.

I may not be illustrious,
   In either Church or State,
But then the reasons obvious,
   My mettle don't inflate.

No thieves have ever stole my purse,
  Somebody calls it trash;
The one that makes that foolish speech
  Has never needed cash.

But there's one thing they freely take,
  And I own it annoys,
When worthless people steal my name
  And give it to their boys.

I am not called combatative.
  But still I want to fight,
When others sign my honest name,
  To silly things they write.

I'm tired of such forgery;
  It wounds my common sense;
Some triflers yet may be hurt
  By me in self defense.

JOHN SMITH.

JONNIE AND I.

My Jonnie and I
" Went down in the rye;"
It may have been wheat,
Or possibly cheat,

Or grass spangled over
With red and white clover.
" At the close of the day,"
When twilight was gray,
We went out to walk,
Or rather to talk—
Please do not ask why—
It is wicked to pry;
We knew our own business,
My Jonnie and I.

———

How time does fly; Jonnie and I,
At close of day in twilight gray,
No more go walking, to do our talking;
We talk at home, nor wish to roam;
While five year Fred and baby Ned,
With prayers all said, are snug in bed—
Surprised are we—who can it be?
Few friends but gay, drop in to say,
Ten years ago this very day
Jonnie and I, without display,
Were married in the good old way.
None ask us why or wish to pry;
We're old folks now, Jonnie and I.

TO THE CHILDREN OF THE SABBATH SCHOOL,

ON THE PRESENTATION OF TESTAMENTS BY THEIR
PASTOR.

Dear children of our special care,
. We're glad to meet you here.
We come with fervency and prayer,
Believing angels near.

Our Pastor, in a hopeful way
Gives each the Testament,
Trusting the Holy Spirit may
Into your hearts be sent.

The Gift of God he cannot give,
Yet it is freely given
To all who will repent and live
The life that leads to heaven.

Eternal life, through Christ, the Son,
Is God's great gift to man.
O, may you each and every one
Accept it while you can!

Now may the Spirit with us bide,
This Children's Day here prove
A precious hallowed Whitsuntide
Of holiness and love.

BREVITIES.

___

LITTLE BOY'S VALENTINE.

Dear, Darling, Little, Sylvia Ann.
> I want to be your lover-man.
> My uncle Bob gave me a sled,
> It's ironed nice and painted red.
> 'Twould fill my heart with honest pride
> To come and take you out to ride.
> So, if you'll go my Valentine,
> Write and I'll come at half past nine.

LITTLE GIRL'S REPLY.

Dear, Precious, Little Bennie Boy,
> 'Twill fill my heart brim full of joy,
> To ride upon your fine new sled,
> All ironed nice and painted red.
> Dear Mamma thinks sure as I go
> You'll tip me over in the snow;
> But Papa says that if you should
> The bath would only do me good.
> So come for sure my Valentine;—
> I wish that now was half past nine!

MOTHER WIT.

No substitute or counterfeit
Can take the place of mother wit;
No culture, sought at great expense,
Atones for lack of common sense.
No trappings gaudy, rich or rare,
Can with a healthy mind compare.

ROBIN REDBREAST.

Little Robin Redbreast coming in the spring.
Little Robin Redbreast, happy little thing!
Little Robin Redbreast hopping on the ground,
Little Robin Redbreast looking all around.
Little Robin Redbreast perching on a rail,
Little Robin Redbreast plump as any quail,
Little Robin Redbreast swinging in a tree,
Little Robin Redbreast looking down at me.
Little Robin Redbreast getting rather high
Little Robin Redbreast, there you go, good-bye!

ALEXANDER.

Alexander the Great,
King of vastest estate!
Drank too much of wine, we know,
And so he died, long, long ago.

LITTLE BOY'S SPEECH.

If I was only wise and good
And many 'Isms understood,
If all of 'Ologies I knew
I would explain them unto you;
If I was gifted, learned and tall,
Instead of awkward, dumb and small,
Then I could speak both loud and clear,
And you would all be glad to hear.
But, as it is, you at me stare,
Saying, "Do see smart Aleck there!"

BESSIE.

Bessie is a pretty girl,
But Bessie is no flirt.
Bessie is a charming girl,
And Bessie's not too pert.
Bessie is not over-wise,
But Bessie's very good;
Who gets our Bessie, gets a prize,
We want that understood.

TO A FLEA.

Wee, restless, bristling, jumping elf,
That never could behave yourself,

Mean, black, back-biting, sneaking pest,
Why can't you let a fellow rest!
Oh! that you were not quite so small,
Then should my vengeance on you fall;
Or, if you were not near so spry,
I'd show you how you had to die.
But as it is I'm in your power,
To be tormented hour by hour.
Tyrant, inventor of distress,
Blood-thirsty, vile and merciless,
I cannot see why you were made;—
Sent here for judgment I'm afraid.
Your only errand seems to be
To aggravate poor souls like me.

RELIGIOUS.

COME, FELLOW-SINNER, COME.

Come, while the church are praying,
  Before the Savior bow;
What gain ye by delaying?
  Accept redemption now.
Think of the preparation;
  The Lamb of God was slain—
Offered for thy salvation:
  And shall it be in vain?
     Come, fellow-sinner, come!

Do wicked thoughts come swarming
  O'er thy awakened heart?
They are the tempter's storming:
  Pray God that fiend depart.
They may come all unbidden;
  Permitted for thy good;
There's evil in thee hidden,
  Thou hast not understood.
     Come, fellow-sinner, come!

Hast thou a morbid longing—
  A sickening, sad unrest—
Do doubts and fears come thronging
  Into thy troubled breast?

Then seek the great Physician:
Plead for His grace and care;
He knows thy lost condition,
And he will answer prayer.
Come, fellow-sinner, come!

Doth sense of guilt come rushing
Through thy unsettled brain;
Are earthly hopes all crushing,
Beneath thy spirit's pain?
List! there's a gentle suing—
A tender, still, small voice;
The Comforter is wooing;
Make now the better choice.
Come, fellow-sinner, come.

ALONE WITH GOD.

When disappointments hover round,
And cherished prospects fail,
When all I see looks dark to me,
My soul is in the vale;
Then let me stray from all away,
And be alone with God.

When those I love the very best
  Don't seem to understand
When this poor dust, in humble trust,
  Seeks comfort at God's hand;
Then it is sweet, at Jesus' feet,
  To be alone with God.

When petty trials swarm about,
  Of which I would not speak,
And woman's tears, like children's fears,
  Show me that I am weak;
Then it is blessed on Christ to rest,
  And be alone with God.

When stern, relentless, frigid death
  Sunders the dearest ties,
When I am left of friends bereft,
  And my sad prayers arise;
Oh! then let me to Jesus flee,
  And be alone with God!

BIBLE COMFORT.

There's comfort in God's holy book,
For such as there for comfort look;
Sweet comfort in his word of grace,
For all who truly seek his face;

Comfort by day, advice by night,
For souls that in his law delight;
Comfort in sickness, pain and woe,
For those who there for comfort go;

Comfort for age, as well as youth,
In this exhaustless fount of truth;
Comfort when we may tempted be,
Jesus was tempted like as we;

When in some weak, unguarded hour
We're baffled by the tempter's power,
Then comfort mitigates the shame,
God understands our feeble frame.

If bowed 'neath sorrow and disgrace,
Like David in Uriah's case,
Soon as we hate and loathe our sin,
Christ sends the comforter within.

'Mid all the anarchy and strife,
Attendant on this present life,
There's comfort in each circumstance,
God's purposes are not by chance,

Comfort, though all of God we see,
Comes darkly through a glass to me;
When, in that holy, happy place,
We shall behold him face to face,

Comfort, all those who enter in,
Will be forever clear of sin,
Will never have another doubt,
And there will be no going out.

NIGHT.

When the sun his course has run,
Tiresome tasks of day are done;
When the whippoorwills are singing,
 Tender, lengthy, joyous lays,
Many insect choirs are ringing
 Gayly out their songs of praise;
While the twilight tints the west,
Ere I seek my needed rest,
Let me too, with fond delight,
Join in praising God at night.

When night's later curtains close
Round me in my safe repose;
While great waterfalls in booming,
 Sound their hallelujahs strong,
Starry heights above them looming,
 Listen to the lofty song;

May I then in lowly way,
Sing as humble sinners may;
Of the mercy, truth and might,
That protecteth through the night.

When my day of time is o'er,
When I toil and sin no more;
When the night of death in coming,
 Finds a present help is near;
Glory lighteth up the gloaming,
 Perfect love ejecteth fear;
When the soul obtains release,
Then is lasting, holy peace,
In the land of pure delight,
Where there is no more of night.

THEY WATCHED HIM THERE.

MATT. XXVII, 36.

Accepting duty as their fate,
Four Roman soldiers, servants of the State,
Stoics, well skilled to do and dare,
Could crucify our Lord, and little care.
Proud soldiers of an Empire great,
Indifferent to Jewish love or hate—
Esteemed it but a tame affair,
To coolly sit them down and watch him there.

But they were doomed strange sounds to hear,
And sights to see that filled their souls with fear,
Earthquake and darkness o'er the land,
Sent deepest terror through this watching band.
Their comprehension was not clear,
Was unknown, angry spirit hov'ring near?
And must they soon before Him stand?
Was sudden, awful vengeance now at hand?

Parting his garments moved them not,
'Twas but a soldier's privilege or lot,
But when they heard his piercing cry,
And saw him meekly bow his head and die,
And thought of his deep plaintive prayer,
In fear they cried the Son of God was there;
He is no culprit, no mere man,
But agent of his God in some great plan.

Jesus now lives to intercede
No heathen guards now watch the spirit freed,
But worldlings watch with evil eye,
His steadfast church below, and taunting try
To find some flaw, some lurking taint,
In every struggling church, and faithful saint,
As watchers mocked our dying Lord,
So now they mock believers in his word.

'Tis well that they such watching do,
For many thus become believers too.
Nor would it hurt the church one whit,
If earth and hell combined were watching it;
Imperfect though his servants be,
Perfection in their risen Lord they see,
Feel that he suffered in their place,
And they are saved by his atoning grace.

STONES ROLLED AWAY.

Impelled by love and sorrow deep,
A band of holy women came to weep,
Choice spices brought to Jesus' grave,
They, too, had trusted that he came to save.
But now their Lord was crucified;
Watching from far they mourned him when he died;
Early they seek his tomb alone,
And wonder "who shall roll away the stone."

They found the stone was rolled away,
Two angels seemed to watch where Jesus lay;
But ah! Methinks they watched as well
These women, and were sent their fears to quell.

Kindly the speaking angel said,
"Why seek ye the living among the dead?
Remember how he spake to you,
He is not here, is risen, lives anew."

An angel's voice, and like a friend,
'Twas strange, and Mary could not comprehend;
But when her Shepherd called her name,
She knew his voice, and glad responses came.
The weaker vessel then was chosen
By Christ to tell his brethren he was risen;
Gladly these honored women went,
The first apostles to apostles sent.

Though now we know our Lord is risen,
And that he ever intercedes in heaven,
Still trials oft obscure our way,
Till we in doubt and fear are led to pray,
And wonder if we are alone,
And who for us "shall roll away the stone."
We're not alone, God hears the call
Of weakest soul that trusts to him its all.

How sweet to think the Lamb once slain
Knows all our love, our hope, our fear, our pain;
And if we are faithful to the end,
Our Elder Brother, Saviour, Lord and Friend,

Will ne'er forsake in trouble's hour,
But will protect by his almighty power,
And in each sad and trying day,
Angels for us will roll the stones away.

LITTLE, BUT GREAT.

A little fire on the hearthstone,
　A little quiet now and then;
A little rest when work is done,
　A little time for book and pen;
Such little things great comfort bring,
And move the grateful heart to sing.

A little precious home of love,
　A little constant quiet cheer;
A little glimpse of things above,
　Blest foretaste, how intensely dear!
And coming in a world like this,
Is earnest of eternal bliss.

A little throwing off of care;
　A little means with want to share;
A little while for thought and prayer,
　A little grace life's woe's to bear:
These little gifts great blessings be,
And sweeten life for more than me.

TWILIGHT.

In the dusky hour of gloaming,
When the cows are homeward coming,
Well clad herd-boy bright and gay,
Follows whistling on his way;
Insects chirping in the grass,
Join the chorus as they pass;
Hireling glad the day is o'er;
Loungers round the village store;
Weary father hasteth home;
Merry children bounding come;
Tell him in their sprightly way,
Haps and mishaps of the day;
Baby's drowsy little head
Finds the couch by mother spread;
Nature seeketh wonted rest;
Beast his lair and bird her nest—
Then my soul, dismiss thy care,
Trusting bow in fervent prayer;
Take from sordid doubt release,
Drink thy fill of proffered peace.

SATISFIED.

Satisfaction cometh not
Though the gifts by earth begot;

East and west, from pole to pole,
Search—Thou canst not find a soul,
Who, 'neath earthly care and strain,
Still remaineth free from pain,
    Or is wholly satisfied!

When we reach the glad forever,
Just beyond the narrow river
That divides this world of ours
From the fair, celestial bowers;
When we see the great white throne;
When we know as we are known;
    We shall then be satisfied.

When, 'mid anthems, we awake
Like our Lord, and for his sake;
When we, washed from all disgrace,
Meet our Maker face to face;
When our heaven-enraptured eyes
See eternal glories rise;
    We shall then be satisfied.

GRACE CONQUERS SELFISHNESS.

When God looked down from heaven and saw
Weak, selfish man transgress his law,
    He had a right, in power and might,

To crush the culprit neath his rod,
And show himself a righteous God.
But mercy, through salvation's plan,
Made pardon possible to man,
    And God be holy still.

The Son, in his unselfishness,
Left heaven, dwelt here, mankind to bless,
    The Book doth tell, we know it well,
Have heard what sacrifice was made;
Know of the price for mortals paid;
Know justice ne'er was satisfied,
'Till Jesus bowed his head and died,
    The just for the unjust.

To us is left the plain command,
Which we, though weak, may understand;
    Go thou, said He, and tell of Me;
Go with unselfishness and prayer,
Proclaim the gospel everywhere,
Lo! I am with you to the end;
Thine elder brother, Saviour, Friend,
    Will needed grace supply.

The bane, the curse of human life:
The moving power in broil and strife,
    Cause of distress, is selfishness.

'Mid high and low' 'mong rich and poor,
In crowded street, on lonely moor,
Where'ere the heart in nature's found,
There doth this hateful trait abound.
    How sad! and yet how true.

When ought of good we undertake,
If any sacrifice we make,
    This lurking sin, rebels within.
E'en when we think it drove away,
Appear it will another way;
And victory is only found
When grace doth more than sin abound.
    To God be all the praise!

Of all the work by mortals done,
None hath been, or will be begun
    In which is less of selfishness
Than in the effort Christians make,
Through love to God and conscience sake,
To tell what they of Jesus know
To every heathen soul below.
    Thrice blessed be the work.

FIFTY YEARS RETROSPECT.

Read at the Semi-Centennial of the Rock Creek Church, Carroll Co. Ind., May 1885.

PART FIRST.

History and tradition say
That fifty years ago to-day,
Age, middle age, and even childhood,
Met in a school house near the wild wood;
Met, and a church was organized,
Of only twenty souls comprised;
And yet that candle-stick has stood,
A banded Christian brotherhood.
God, with a parent's tender care,
Had sent a chosen vessel there,
To preach, to counsel, and to pray, •
As his enlightened servants may.
The Spirit with redeeming power,
Hallowed the consecrated hour:
And Christ himself was there to bless
The worship in the wilderness.
We seem to see them as they meet,
From time to time for service sweet;
Coming from many miles around,
With purpose firm and faith profound,

Coming alone; coming in mass,
O'er ways extremely hard to pass;
Coming each other's hand to take,
With honest, friendly, hearty shake.
Their lonely lot had set aglow
A friendship we may never know,
Had waked a longing of the heart
That other scenes do not impart.
The house of logs was rude and new,
The floor was rough, the windows few,
The door was open left for light,
The ample hearth with fire was bright—
For wood was plenty in those days
Of simple, sturdy, homely ways;
And fire would drive out damp and chill,
And throw a light more ruddy still.
Most of that band have passed away,
But three remain with us to-day,
Yet when the just attain their rest
Their memories are ever blest.

PART SECOND.

Once in the joyous winter time,
When sleigh-bells lent a merry chime,

And all the ground was white with snow,
In days of thirty years ago—
One Sabbath morning bright and clear,
A guest came up to worship here.
That was the first thy handmaid knew
Of hereabout, this church, or you.
Not to log school house then we came,
But to a little church of frame,
Nor was it like this house to-day,
But far more humble in its way—
With truth, and sentiments expressed,
How was the stranger's mind impressed?
Simply service appropriate,
Beyond that, no impression great,
Except, emotions strange and strong,
Awakened by the power of song,
Grand in its sacred melody,
And depths of rare intensity.
For twenty years this band had stood.
A monument that God was good,
When flesh grew weak and love lukewarm,
And even in the night of storm,
When adverse winds of earth were blowing,
The faithful few who toiled in rowing,

Ever, in answer to their cry,
Had heard the cheering "It is I."

PART THIRD.

To-day we meet to retrospect;
On past and present to reflect.
To note a heavenly Father's love,
And forward look to rest above.
Dejection, with complaining tears,
Says, Little done in fifty years;
Behold the prevalence of sin,
Then think of good that might have been
Had this one church done as it should,
It's every member all he could.
Nay! Nay! says Charity, Forbear;
Vain MIGHT HAVE BEENS produce despair;
Look truth and justice in the face,
Use honest candor in the case,
And then decide what would have been,
Whether the more or less of sin—
Had this same Church been swept away,
Fifty full years ago to-day;
Entirely blotted out from the earth,
The day of its organic birth.

Its hope, its zeal, all laid away;
Nor ordinance on Holy Day;
Its hymns and anthems left unsung,
No careful training of the young,
No thoughtful deeds of Christian care,
No fervent all prevailing prayer,
No gifts for any worthy Board,
Nor consecration to the Lord—
Not so; God kept this Church alive,
Forgave its sins, caused it to thrive,
Gave special gifts his servants craved,
Added of such as should be saved—
Glory on earth, glory in heaven,
To God be all the Glory given!
Let men and angels join and raise
United, ardent, endless praise.

INNER CHAMBER.

In peaceful quiet of one's room,
   With all the world shut out,
Blest be the throwing off of gloom
   And casting out of doubt.

Weary with earthly toil and care,
How sweet doth rest appear;
Precious the privilege of prayer
When only God may hear.

Truly one day within his courts
Excels a thousand spent
In worldly vanity and sports,
Ending in discontent.

When two or three together meet,
Intent on praise and prayer,
Then sacred fellowship is sweet,
For Christ is with them there.

But every Christian soul hath want
Peculiarly his own,
Supplied by grace's exhaustless fount,
When with his God alone.

MISSION FIRE.

There was a joyful sound in heaven, and loud
And clear the holy hallelujahs rang,
Angels and archangels sang;

And God's elect on earth beheld a cloud
    Of promise, and though small, they understood
    A fire was kindled that betokened good.
That fire was foreign missions, and they saw,
    With faith and hope and fond desire,
That it was lighted by no broken law,
    But gospel love and zeal had lit the fire.

Great powers of earth and hell conspired anon
    With blackest heathen darkness, fear and doubt,
    To quell, to quench and wholly to put out
This sacred fire, which, praised be God, burned on;
    At first with seeming weakness and but slow,
    Yet their was life eternal in its glow;
Blood, blood, pure, consecrated blood was shed,
    And freely, blindly poured upon the fire,
Orphans and widows wailing for the dead;
    Yet still the fire burned on brighter and higher.

Satan then poured upon and all about
    The fire, cold, smothering, damp indifference;
    Smouldering, it bravely strove in self-defence,
Flickered, revived, burned on but went not out.
    "Great is the mystery of godliness."
    Jesus was ever near the fire to bless,

Pouring the "oil of joy for mourning" there,
  Protecting by his all-sufficient power,
Hearing and answering each fervent prayer,
  And ne'er forsaking, for a single hour.

Protected thus, the fire burned on, and will,
  Till nations all shall know and fear the Lord.
  Behold the fullness of his gracious word:
The knowledge of our God the earth shall fill;
  Darkness before the light shall pass away,
  Gross heathen darkness turn to Christian day,
The cause of Christ will more and more advance,
  Till to the Son be made a full consession
Of heathen lands for an inheritance,
  And utmost parts of earth for a possession.

PRAYER FOR KINDRED.

Father, I feel that I am thine;
Have sweet assurance Christ is mine;
Yet I have an unanswered prayer,
That fills my longing soul with care.

I have enough of worldy good,
My friends attend me as they should;
My cup with blessings runneth o'er,
And yet I crave one blessing more.

For kindred and relation's sake.
My heart and soul are all awake;
I pray, O Lord, that I may be
A help in leading them to thee.

Give me the wisdom and the grace
To fill a humble Christian's place;
And grant the dear ones in my home
May to a waiting Savior come.
I have the faith it will be so;
Indeed, it seems I almost know.
Dear father, grant the boon I crave
Through Him who died the lost to save.

WHERE IS LIBERTY?

But little liberty we find—
   Ours is a servile lot,
Not much of freedom for mankind,
   And they desire it not.

Man only asks freedom in this—
   To serve what he loves most;
Then calls that liberty and bliss
   A thing of which to boast.

No mind is apt to soar above
   Enjoyment it can see
In dearest object of its love,
   Whate'er that object be. .

But human tastes diverge so wide—
   What one could serve and trust,
Another mortal would decide
   An object of disgust.

Some blindly serve a fellow-man,
   And help him gather pelf;
Another will condense his plan,
   And labor for himself.

The libertine's best hopes are sold
   And sacrificed to lust;
The miser gives his life for gold—
   He loves the shining dust.

How many slaves of appetite
   Go sadly down and fast,
Till early manhood ends in blight—
   Freedom and life are past.

Ambition, drunk with love of fame,
   Treats freedom with abuse;

And fashion's fitful, gaudy game
  Leaves it quite out of use.

For all who follow in their train
  Leave liberty behind;
Receive as wages only pain,
  Or vanity of mind.

Bondage, bondage, on every side,
  And profitless we see!
Until we near our Saviour hide,
  Then he will make us free.

And though our foes may rushing come,
  The storm will soon be past,
When God himself doth take us home
  To liberty at last.

AGED CHRISTIAN'S SOLILOQUY.

With earthly scenes I'm almost through,
And I am glad and sorry too;
Glad to be done with toil and strife,
Sorry I've erred so oft in life.

Glad from temptation to be free,
Sorry it yet o'ercometh me;

Glad I shall soon be clear of sin,
Sorry it still doth lurk within.

Glad, when I reach the shining shore,
I'll greet the loved ones gone before;
Sorry the view, so strangely dear,
Should dimly to my sight appear.

Glad for the hope that cheereth me,
That I shall soon my Saviour see;
Then perfect love, and constant joy,
Will leave no sorrow to annoy.

EASTER EVEN.

The forty days of Lent were passed,
    And now the Easter even
Came wafted in on balmy winds,
    Reminding us of heaven.

We sat within the dear old church,
    So fondly claimed as ours;
Sat waiting for the white-robed priest,
    'Amid perfume and flowers.

When softly through the wide church door
    Came one not there for years;

His presence wakened memories
That moistened eyes with tears.

Oft there with wife and children,
We'd seen him in his prime;
Had joined with him in Zion's songs
And prayers at Easter time.

In distant village long he'd dwelt,
Bereft of service sweet;
And his one longing hope had been
With us once more to meet.

So now he came at Easter time;
Took us by sad surprise;
For even at a glance we saw
That sightless were his eyes.

A daughter held his trembling hand,
Guided his feeble feet,
With quiet carefulness and love,
To his remembered seat.

The service cheered his stricken heart;
His woe gave place to weal;
And every soul that worshipped there
Was moved to greater zeal.

The western sun came beaming in,
    Illumed the flowers and wall,
Sending a mellow, peaceful light
    O'er priest, blind guest and all.

A holy calmness filled the place :
    A joyful earnest given;
Saying, be faithful to the end,
    None will be blind in heaven.

LINES WRITTEN FOR THE DEDICATION OF A PARSONAGE.

Say not man's strength or woman's tact
    Reared this good house wherein we stand,
'Twas built by condescending act
    Of God with his Almighty hand.

Nor think our pastor, learned and wise,
    Through eloquence and manly power,
Caused these accepted walls to rise,
    God also nerved him for the hour.

What has been done was done by prayer,
    And we have truly learned to know
Who prays the most, does best his share,
    Since faith and works together go.

We felt a galling sense of cares,
  Our work was being poorly done,
Therefore we went requesting prayers
  Of dear aunt Martha Williamson.

"Ah, yes," said she, "Go on your way,
At home I on my knees will pray."

Thus blest we left her hallowed door,
Parted to meet on earth no more.

And while in unity to-night,
  We're grateful for one more success,
She in the realms of endless light,
  Lives in eternal happiness.

Are we prepared to meet her there?
  Do faith and works in us combine?
And are we prevalent in prayer?
  God grant this be thy state and mine.

DIDST THOU REMEMBER?

When all was gay, in fond array,
Upon our own Thanksgiving day,
Glad hours passed swiftly on their way—
  Didst thou remember then the poor?

When lively chime and pleasant rhyme
Proclaimed at merry Christmas time,
Good news for every land and clime,
   Didst thou remember then the poor?

When New Year's light declared it right,
And happy children, gay and bright,
Caroled in lays of pure delight,
   Didst thou remember then the poor?

They yet are here, with prospects drear,
Thou hast neglected them, we fear;
If so, thy duty still is clear:
   Though late, remember now the poor!

PRODIGAL SONS.

Few are the flocks, though choice the stock,
   But one black sheep is there;
Fewer the homes, though guarded well,
   Where no bad child brings care.

There is sorrow greater than
   The sorrow for the dead;
When sore and bleeding parent hearts
   Mourn children's honor fled.

Then let us weep resignedly
   For little nestlings flown;
God pity those who sadder weep,
   For sons rebellious grown.

Phinehas, Hophni and Absalom,
   Condemned in holy page,
Have living representatives
   In each successive age.

Full many are the prodigals
   That never do repent,
And many young and blooming forms
   To shameful graves are sent.

Frail forms are bent, gray heads are bowed,
   Fond hearts are broke by grief;
And parents humbly pray, that death
   May bring their souls relief.

How sad to own that this is so,
   Yet so it is the same;
And God in his omnisciency,
   Knows whose and where's the blame.

DYING TO-NIGHT.

Going to night a father said,
And bowed his reverential head;
Going to die this very night,
Going now, and ready quite.
Dying with suffocating pain,
With pressed and agonizing brain;
Still nothing can my soul affright,
'Twill all be over yet to-night.
A sudden tremor cometh now,
And death-sweat standeth on my brow,
Yet all around me seemeth bright—
Just think, this is my last sad night!
Here, daughter, close beside me stand,
Well, kiss your dying father's hand;
Yes, breathe a prayer so soft and low
That none but we and God can know.
A sudden hush, and nothing more,
Without a struggle all is o'er,
We gaze transfixed upon the spot—
Say, is this death, or is it not?
A calm and peaceful marble brow,
A weary body rested now;
If this be death, then death is blest,
A Christian ent'ring into rest.

TRUST.

How sweet to trust in those we love,
  And firmly to believe;
Our household treasures are above
  The mass that would deceive.

'Tis well to trust in friends we find
  By nature not so near;
Whom fellow feeling maketh kind,
  And kindred spirit dear.

All this is comforting and right,
  For tenants of the sod;
But naught can make our lives so bright
  As humble trust in God.

Mere human pillars are at best
  Finite and insecure;
But souls who trust in God, are blest
  With fortress firm and sure.

TIRED.

Too tired to work, to talk or play,
Too tired to even think or pray,
Except in feebleness to say
  Father, thy will be done,

Tired of earth's metal and alloy;
Tired of its paltry show and joy;
Tired of some people who annoy,
    Yes, almost tired of self.

Tired while at home, more so away;
Tired of the customs of the day;
Tired of their bombast and display;
    Oh! why are mortals vain?

Tired of the day, tired of the night,
Tired of the shadow, and the light,
Tired of uncertainty and blight;
    But not of Christian hope.

Tired of the heat, tired of the cold,
Tired out with growing weak and old;
But never tired of being told,
    There's perfect rest in heaven.

SABBATH EVENING.

One more day of rest is done,
Sacred hours forever gone;
Deepening shades of evening fall,
Shadows dance upon the wall,

Softly darkness fills the room;
Not the darkness born of gloom—
Simply curtailing of night;
While there comes a vision bright,
O'er the spirit wrapt in thought,
O'er the soul by Jesus bought;
Faith beholds the better land,
Where the saints acquitted stand;
Holy, heavenly joys are seen,
And the ransomed spirit clean,
Resting with the sinner's Friend,
Where the Sabbaths never end.

WORKING WOMEN.

My friends, I've been thinking, and thinking again,
Of Jesus' commandment to women and men;
How plainly he bade us his gospel proclaim,
To work in his vineyard and honor his name.

It came not from mortal, this binding command,
By infinite wisdom the great work was planned;
Then let us each try this command to fulfill,
By aiding the work with a hearty good will.

Both Lois and Eunice were workers I see;
Phebe was a servant, and so should we be;

Priscilla did her work, so should you and I—
The heathen send us Macedonia's cry.

Dorcas was commended for work in her day,
Frank Lydia oft met her companions to pray;
And Persis, who labored so much in the Lord,
With Paul is now reaping eternal reward.

God loveth the worker that in giving delights,
The widow was lauded for giving her mites;
And oft he requires us on others to wait,
Like vigilant Rhoda who stood at the gate.

Mary knew Jesus, though a Thomas could doubt,
Damaris was constant, if scoffers did scout;
And of the chief women, there were not a few
Who set good example for me and for you.

Christ said one meek woman had done what she could,
And this was accounted unto her for good,
So, however humble our duty may be,
That is the right pathway for you and for me.

Oh, let us be women of consciences clear,
Let us pray for the love that casteth out fear,
Then working for Jesus will prove a delight,
The yoke is so easy, the burden so light.

OUR MINISTER'S TWO WIVES.

Our minister was wise, though young,
His harp with many strings was strung,
And sweetly Zion's songs he sung.

His wife was modest and shamefaced,
Young, beautiful, demure and chaste,
A helpmeet suited to his taste.

They came among us, as they should,
Fully intent on doing good;
And, as they thought, well understood.

But soon sister Insinuate,
Who never tells a matter straight,
Was hinting at a dreadful rate.

And then Samantha Anna Tattle,
Determined she would give them battle,
And boisterously her tongue did rattle.

She said she was surprised to find
The wife had such a narrow mind;
And was to worldliness inclined.

Gossip disliked her haughty look;
Had caught her with a story book;
Felt confident she could not cook.

Meanwhile the frail, confiding wife,
Suspecting naught of guile or strife,
Aimed at a high and holy life.

Shielded her youth had been from toil,
From disaffection and turmoil;
And little had she seen of broil.

So when she was not understood,
And evil was returned for good,
She failed; no wonder that she should.

With nerves unequal to the strain,
Hers was a life of constant pain;
Yet in no ear did she complain.

At last in sudden, quiet way,
To realms of everlasting day
The weary spirit passed away.

The Church, staggered by sad surprise,
Then shut its criticising eyes,
And said we were unkind, unwise.

Her stricken parents, weeping, come;
Cling to the body, take it home;
Our minister returns alone.

Sad, very sad, but reconciled,
He lives, God's pure, submissive child,
Growing each day more meek and mild.

Man was not made to dwell alone;
A minister should have a home,
Another wife must to us come.

This time the Church selects the spouse;
Must see him solemnize his vows,
And notice how his consort bows.

But soon they found that nod was law;
She could detect the slightest flaw,
And plainly tell the faults she saw.

She showed how gifted women pray;
But with such polish and display,
Most of our girls were drove away.

And if they guidance sought in prayer,
It must have been some other where,
They found no fellow-feeling there.

She kept church matters like a clock;
Her steady nerves received no shock.
Could she not manage one small flock?

In age a fever laid her low;
We saw at first that she would go;
Nor of the going did she know.

Though she had been with us for years,
We felt like subjects more than peers;
And for her shed not many tears.

The organ played a mournful song;
A D.D. preached profoundly strong,
And wrote obituary long.

Our minister, easily consoled,
Greatly endeared to young and old,
Waits till a few more days are told.

EASTER HYMN.

Sing songs of glad hosannas now,
    The Crucified is risen;
In joyful adoration bow,
    As do the hosts of heaven.

The God of grace and glory lives,
    The Truth, the Light, the word;
Pardon and free salvation gives
    To lovers of the Lord.

The meek and lowly Lamb is King,
Nor sleeps he in the grave;
Let anthems loud the welkin ring:
He reigns the lost to save.

"Because I live, ye to shall live"—
This promise firm and sure,
He doth to all believers give,
Who to the end endure.

How blest the hope that even we
May win the offered prize;
May be at last from sin set free;
May, like our Savior, rise.

MY NEIGHBOR.

He sat down in my open door,
Just as he'd often done before,
A calm look on his aged face,
I felt 'twas the effect of grace;
For this wise, Christian neighbor true
Years of affliction had passed through.

'Isms and 'ologies too free
I have allowed to trouble me;

The Church, I argue, is enough,
All other bands are empty puff;
Orders and clans and worldly creeds
Are nothing that a Christian needs.

The funeral on yesterday
Was an affair of great display;
Can you endure such things? said I,
The folly must your spirit try;
How can they wish to make a show
When a dear friend is lying low?

I did not like it, to be sure,
Still I had nothing to endure;
For I have learned one thing, said he,
What I can't help, to let it be.
God will protect, I have no fear,
As long as I've a conscience clear.

I knew his words were pure gold,
Both fitly spoken and well told;
My neighbor's eye I'll let alone,
While I've a beam within my own;
I've learned how one pure soul can rest
In peace that I have not possessed.

MONDAY MORNING.

Pleasant or storming, no forlorning Monday morning
At break of day, up and away, without delay.
The Sabbath's rest, holy and blest, gives strength
and zest
For honest toil, without turmoil, or sordid broil.
Work on this plan, do what you can, for God and man.
Then up, away, without delay, 'tis working day.

WAKING.

Waking in sacred hush of night,
    Assured that all is well,
Our thanks ascend with calm delight,
    To God in whom we dwell.
Waking 'mid home surroundings dear,
    With no discord to chafe,
While a protecting God is near,
    We rest content and safe.

Waking with morn's returning light,
    Refreshed by peaceful sleep,
Believing he who kept through night,
    To end of days will keep.

If earthly wakings thus are blest,
  And blest they are, we know,
God's children many can attest
  That they have found them so.

What must the heavenly waking be
  When sleep of death is o'er;
We wake our Saviour's face to see,
  And wake to sin no more.
Waking from all temptation free,
  Our every want supplied,
And waking with his likeness, we
  Shall then be satisfied.

THISTLES, NOT FIGS.

It was my lot, some years ago,
To live where many thistles grow;
Long months they sleep beneath the snow;
When it is gone, begin to show.

They grow in every field and lane,
On towering hill and sloping plain;
Farmers there try, but try in vain,
To keep the thistles from the grain.

The seeds go flying through the air,
Wafted on breezes everywhere,
And when they light, if soil is there,
They spring up rank as any tare.

No figs on any thistle grow;
That fact was settled long ago,
And in a moral sense we know
No thistle doth a fig bestow.

The seeds of error, shame and doubt,
By evil means are strewn about;
God grant clear heads, pure hearts and stout,
May keep these moral thistles out.

The bristling stirrer up of strife,
Whose words are piercing as a knife,
Though his prescriptions may be rife,
Can heal no boil, prolong no life.*

But he who tries mankind to bless
In serving God finds happiness,
And humbly doth his sins confess:
That soil yields fruits of righteousness.

*2 Kings xx. 7. Is. xxxviii. 21.

MY LITTLE RED CLOAK.

In dear home comfort long ago,
'Mid evergreens, rocks, hills and snow,
A nervous, peevish child lived I,
Who often laid awake to cry
When things went wrong, or as I thought,
Were not progressing as they ought.

I had a red merino cloak,
Made with a Mother Hubbard yoke.
Not elegant or high of price,
It yet was very warm and nice.

But soon my ever restless brain,
Which could not long be free from pain,
Discovered ere another fall
That precious cloak would be too small.

I knew my parents could provide;
No needed gift would be denied;
That they were able to protect,
Nor ever guilty of neglect.

Yet then and there came keen distress,
Which I took care not to express,
Choosing to bear the pain alone,
Rather than have my folly known.

Though small, I knew 'twas mean and weak
Of those distrustful thoughts to speak.

Next fall I had a better wrap,
Matching a well-becoming cap;
And 'twas a joy, not cross to me,
From my old mantle to be free.

So God's own children must confess
They borrow trouble and distress,
Clinging to out-grown carnal cloaks,
With ugly, ill-befitting yokes.

They shrink, and dread to put away
The earthly covering of clay;
Forget that blood-washed garments fair
Alone can match the crowns they'll wear.

Backslide and merit only shame:
Yet he who knows their feeble frame,
Still woos them by his Spirit's might,
And fits at last for robes of white.

God grant that each of us and all
Grow till our earthly garments small
Are changed for those of broader love,
Worn round our Father's throne above.

IN MEMORY OF PHILIP HINKLE.

Threescore years and ten, save one,
Were passed before his work was done.
Diligence marked his business life
With fervency devoid of strife.
At last no fever racked his brain,
Nor slow decline, with nights of pain.
God laid death's finger on his heart,
And said, "Freed soul, in peace depart."
The high and low together mourn,
And elder brother from them borne;
And, though he sang himself to sleep,
What wonder that his friends should weep?
They miss the loving spirit flown,
Are comforted and not alone.
God gave, and, bless his holy name,
He hath a right to take the same.

HEALING BALM.

The golden bowl is broken,
   My baby's gone before,
The last adieu is spoken,
   She's reached the painless shore.

A pang is through me darting
  That seems the soul to sound,
The dreadful sting of parting,
  Keen, sacred, and profound.

Friends show the kindest feeling,
  Their sympathy is free,
But Christ can do the healing,
  He hath the balm for me.

Then freely I'll apply it;
  So sorely I'm bereft,
He never will deny it:
  I have a Saviour left.

Although he dwells in glory,
  He sends me comfort here;
I read the "old, old story"
  And feel that he is near.

AFTER HOLIDAYS.

Thanksgiving, Christmas and New Year's all o'er,
Duties confront us, as they did before;
Duties demanding immediate care,
Calling for sacrifice, labor and prayer.

After the holidays, cometh reaction;
Home comfort hath a peculiar attraction;
Quietude bringeth serene meditation
On God's most wonderful plan of salvation.

After the holidays, many are blest
With animation imparted by rest;
May God's own mercy reach other hearts drear,
Whom holidays brought but pitiful cheer.

After the holidays, comes soul inspection,
That faults may receive their proper correction;
While hearts with tender emotions are warm,
Is time for needed and thorough reform.

After the holidays, sin doth remain;
Still are we cumbered with sorrow and pain
But, as by one man came sin and the fall,
So one sacrifice provideth for all.

TEMPTATION.

Temptation, thing detestable.
That lures us on to grief,
Adam and Eve, I do believe,
Thought it of troubles chief.

And every erring child of theirs
  Hath felt its baneful power,
By it hath been led into sin
  In an unguarded hour.

Not simply during youthful days
  Are mortals led astray,
But through this life of care and strife
  We need to watch and pray.
The tempter learns our weakest point,
  Then hurls allurements in,
By wily art ensnares the heart
  Through our besetting sin.

God never tempteth any soul,
  'Tis Satan and our lust.
God hears the call of one and all
  Who in his name will trust.
Blest be the man who can endure
  Temptation, clear of sin,
In trial's hour he hath the power
  That grace imparts within.

Let him who thinketh that he stands
  Take heed lest he may fall.
In time of fear let us draw near,
  And on our Saviour call.

The Rock of Ages never swerves
   'Neath any tempting blast;
Souls anchored there by faith and prayer
   Will rest secure at last.

OUR GOSPEL.

Rejoice, rejoice, with heart and powers;
The gospel of our Lord is ours.
Not yours, while I remain in doubt.
Nor mine, still leaving you without;
But ours, and there is waiting still
Good news for whosoever will
Repent, call humbly on the Lord,
Accept his grace and trust his word.
But heathen souls, in dark distress,
Grope for the light that we possess;
How can they call in word or thought.
On him of whom they are not taught?
How learn they, saving teacher teach?
How hear, excepting preacher preach?
And who shall preach ere he be sent?
Who warn the nations to repent?
Who under God can send like we?
To whom the gracious gift is free,

A gift we may not comprehend,
Can not, till time with us shall end?
This much we feel, that every man
Doth need to know the gospel plan,
Ere steadfast hope and Godly fear
Can fit for christian service here,
Or saving faith and grateful love
Prepare for endless rest above.
Hence, duty calls us to explain
Why Christ the Lamb of God was slain,
And bids us labor, watch and pray,
Trusting our precious gospel may
Soon earth o'erspread, nor be denied
To souls for whom the Savior died.

BESTIR THYSELF.

"When thou hearest the sound of a going in the tops of the mulberry
trees, then thou shalt bestir thyself."—2 Sam. v. 24.

In the valley of giants the Philistines were spread,
When David again inquiringly said,
"Shall I go up to them, encamped as they stand?
Lord, wilt thou deliver them into mine hand?"

"Thou shalt not confront them," the Lord then
replied;
"Encompass behind them, advance as I guide;

When I move before thee, rest not in the lees;
Bestir at the sound in the mulberry trees."

And David obeying smote them at command;
The host shrank before him unable to stand;
From Geba to Gazer they fled in dismay;
The Lord by his presence deciding the day.

God moves on before us in these latter days;
In mighty, unsearchable, glorious ways;
Wide far distant regions in heathenish night
Are ready, yea waiting and calling for light.

Tried veterans with wisdom have compassed about;
Discerned weakest places, within and without;
In many encounters have victory won,
By strength of the Spirit, through faith in the Son.

Bestir thyself, soldier; bestir thyself, saint;
Take courage, ye weary; revive now, ye faint;
On highland, on lowland, on isles of the seas,
There's a sound in the tops of the mulberry trees.

But who for the work is sufficiently strong?
For service so wearing, for conflict so long.
God's wonderful movings! how strange in our eyes—
With weak things of earth he confoundeth the wise.

Frail woman, weak woman's a place in the plan;
A place that can never be filled by a man;
Bestir thyself, woman; we've learned by degrees,
There's a moving for thee in the mulberry trees.

Have we not a valley of Rephaim to-day;
Where evil encampeth, intending to stay?
List! from the great west comes a wail on the breeze,
Methinks is a sound in the mulberry trees.

Then think of waste places all over our land,
Where victims of error benightedly stand—
Bestir thyself, Christian, whoever ye be;
The master is moving, and calleth for thee.

MISCELLANEOUS.

OUT OF HIS SPHERE.

We've heard and reheard, and then heard it o'er,
Till our spleen rises at hearing it more,
That woman is useful, happy and dear,
Only while she remains in her sphere.

But man leaves his sphere as much as his mate,
His love of adventure being as great;
Weaker her vessel, more fragile and fair,
His bark as often goes down in despair.

John Jones, the farmer, and Susan his wife,
Useful and happy, grow thrifty in life.
John Jones turned banker, quite out of his sphere,
Loses his fortune in less than a year.

Vender, M. Salesman, in his father's store,
Proves just the element needed before;
But since his visit at grandmother's farm,
He thinks to manage that place like a charm.

So Salesman senior hands over the cash,
Junior starts farming with wonderful dash;
Though scientific, he nothing can clear,
'Cause the young tradesman is out of his sphere.

Painwell Physician whose consummate skill
Plies all the marvels of powder and pill;
Became excited one politic year,
So off he went whirling out of his sphere.

Peter Preceptor seemed firm as a rock,
Running his school almost like a clock;
Till a vain longing for clerical cheer,
Finally hustled him out of his sphere.

Oh, man born of woman, when will you know
This world is tinseled for vanity's show;
You need not go roving, time is too dear,
Stick to your business, not leaving your sphere.

MEN'S RIGHTS.

I have pondered and thought and still do not know,
Why people will wander and run about so—
Will waste their strength daily, and lose their sleep
      nights,
Declaring that women shall have their just rights.

That they have their just rights, is clear to my mind,
Though woes and afflictions we always shall find;
They are but the result of our fallen state,
I doubt not Eve's sorrows were fully as great.

The first pair of culprits went skulking away;
When brought before justice had little to say ;
When banished from Eden, their sentence was plain,
Man must endure labor, and women bear pain.

From that day till this there has been no reprieve,
And there never will be, in time, we believe;
But in the long-reaching original plan,
God deigned to give some rights to poor fallen man.

His grand right of ruler is blended with toil;
He sweats his brow, working the God accursed soil;
He has right to provide, to plan and to save;
This makes life a struggle from cradle to grave.

Man has sacred right to the help-meet God gave,
And for whose support he is willing to save—
A right to the confidence, love and respect.
Of her whom he giveth his years to protect.

Does man get his just rights? not always I fear;
And is woman's conscience in this respect clear?
Since men are their patrons—by nature they are,
Let women prove faithful by treating them fair.

THE VAIN CRITIC'S SOLILOQUY.

Most mortals are afraid of me,
Fine critic of no low degree.
Those who are not, I'll teach to see
That they, by far, had better be.

I have a self appointed task;
And no promotion do I ask;
I deign to wear no shield or mask,
But in bold self-assurance bask.

When I with dignity inflate,
Display myself in best estate,
My friends admire my happy fate,
And nobly try to imitate.

And though my rivals underrate;
They try their best to emulate ;
While enemies, despite their hate,
Have to acknowledge I am great.

GRUMBLING.

Grumbling gives pain like cute disease,
    And it is chronic, too;
The victim you can never please,
    No matter what you do.

He suffers with a constant dread,
　And aggravation great,
Lest something will be done or said
　Too early or too late.

He seems to feel the keenest pain
　In looking at the sky—
And thinks that it will surely rain,
　Or else will be too dry.

He mourns his neighbor's honor flown—
　They borrow, vex and plot;
And what is his, and his alone,
　They've kept, and feign forgot.

The sermons are too dreadful long,
　The singing is too fast;
The Sabbath-school's a babel throng,
　Its usefulness is past.

He's sorry the prayer-meeting is
　A-growing rather thin;
Had it not been for him, and his,
　Extinct it would have been.

He says that no one else can know
　His full extent of pain;
Sickness and sorrow, grief and woe,
　He bears, but don't complain.

WITH GLADNESS.

Serve the Lord with gladness,
　Be merry while you may;
Anticipate not sadness,
　Sufficient is its day.

Serve the Lord with gladness,
　Rejoicing evermore;
Fret not for other's badness,
　"Twas ever so of yore.

Serve the Lord with gladness,
　His mercies forget not;
He sendeth you no sadness
　Beyond the common lot.

Serve the Lord with gladness,
　Submissive bear the rod;
Repining would be madness,
　Rejoice that he is God.

HANDSOME.

Handsome is, that handsome does;
　Repeat it o'er and o'er;
For every time it's told to us,
　We realize it more.

A truer maxin than this one,
　Methinks I'm never told;
Nor seems it much the worse for wear,
　Though growing rather old.

Staid, honest, useful homely dames,
　Par excellence will pass;
The maid of sense and modesty,
　Is deemed a charming lass;
Indeed, it is the wide world o'er,
　As with your friends and you;
Plain worthy people fairer seem,
　Than vicious beauties do.

SAD, SAD HOME.

Some truths are very, very strange,
　Some homes are strangely sad,
And one at least was past the range
　Of ordinary bad.

Rachel, when young, was beautiful,
　Possessed of healthful glow,
While conduct kind and dutiful
　Rendered her doubly so.

She never was angelic pure,
  Had not so far to fall;   •
But how she fell, and to what depths,
  Is saddening to recall.

Early she loved and wed with one
  Who sought her as a prize;
While doting friends believed his choice
  Both fortunate and wise.

They were not either high or low
  In city's gilded strife;
But plainer aristocracy
  In frugal country life.

At first both taste and comfort blessed
  Their pleasant rural home,
And none foresaw that misery
  Through drunkenness would come.

Slowly and stealthily it came;
  Nor in the common way—
Not he, but she wrought ruin there,
  By drinking day by day.

The husband died ere any knew
    The full extent of shame,
The utter infamy and blight
    That o'er his household came.

With charity's thick mantle he
    Her fault had covered o'er;
The reckless widow boldly drank
    Not less, but more and more,

Her friends and his, hoping reform,
    Helped him to hide her shame;
Confounded and discouraged, now
    They few and fewer came.

Her one surviving wayward child,
    The widow's only son,
Went swiftly in the downward course,
    Neglected and undone.

Their home became a sordid den
    Of drunkenness and sin;
Neglect, decay and sloth without,
    Squalor and strife within.

She lived to see her boy laid low
  Within a drunkard's grave,
Yet sought no spmpathy of man,
  Nor called on God to save.

Weeping she gazed upon her dead,
  Then stupid grew and dumb;
Her conscience, heart and intellect
  Were all consumed by rum.

And when she laid her down to die
  How did her spirit grope!
Nothing to bind her to this world,
  And for the next, no hope.

Say not this is not true, for true it is;
How many times I know not, but once 'twas so :
I heard, I saw, I grieve to know it true.

HUMBUG.

I'm humbug of a high degree,
And everybody's pleased with me,
A happy fate has made me great,
  I am no common pug;
Although the dictionary says,
  That I'm a vulgar bug.

I'm older than that boastful book,
    Which claims to know so much;
And it is only English prose,
    While I can charm in Dutch.
    But, patent right is my delight;
    Oh! what a grand display
I make in showing it about,
    In my impressive way.
There's not a nation on the earth
    That is not fond of me;
Nor has there been in ages past,
    And there will never be.
They pay me cash, to cut a dash,
    And treat me like a king;
Whether I lecture wonder'ly,
    Or hire a girl to sing.
It's all the same, I have the game,
    And all the people shout:
Hurra, Professor Humbug is
    The greatest man that's out.

THE DESERTED HOMESTEAD.

Though more a mansion than a cot,
It seems just like a thing forgot;

Discordant sound disturbs it not,
Nor lively echo cheers the spot.

Oppressive silence hovers round,
Stern, frigid, dismal and profound;
This house and this neglected ground
Was once all prevalent with sound.

It seems to me but yesterday,
Since the old home, now in decay,
Was filled with children bright and gay,
And I a child with them at play.

No footstep now is in the hall;
Empty each room both large and small;
From garrett to the lowest wall
Deep gloom o'erspreads it like a pall,

Gone, gone! Beyond the least repair,
No mortal deigns to give it care;
No joy, no hope may enter there,
It stands an emblem of despair.

THE QUAKERESS' DREAM.

I'll tell you a story, which is nothing more,
I dare to presume, than you've heard before;
But if you have heard it, 'tis no matter then,
'Twill not take you long to hear it again.

A good Quaker lady of Heavenly mind
Was nevertheless to smoking inclined,
And as she grew older, and every day better,
This troublesome practice, did her more enfetter.

This lady was thoughtful, and very discreet,
And her meditation of Heaven was sweet;
But strange! as she grew more happy in grace,
The pipe grew more firmly attached to her face.

One night being weary, not able to sleep,
Her meditations grew solemn and deep;
She said I'm not well, a solace I need,
I'll sit up in bed and puff at the weed.

With smoke curling gracefully 'bove her night-cap,
Soon the old lady fell into a nap;
She dreamed she had trod the road narrow and
    straight,
And now she was safe at the Heavenly gate.

She thought that she said to the angel in white,
Please, Sir, let me in? you'll find it all right,
I will said the angel, with kindest of look,
As soon as I find your name in the book.

The angel came back with a sorrowful face,
Your name is not there, I've looked in each place.
She said, look again, I'm sure it is there,
My life has been one of faith, and hope and prayer.

Again with much patience the angel did look,
Again could not find her name in the book;
The lady grew frantic, Oh! am I deceived
Do look once again, 'tis their I believe.

The angel seemed moved to witness her pain
And willingly went on his errand again,
And when he returned, he smiled as he spoke,
I've found it at last—all covered with smoke.

The lady awoke, and I've heard it said
She ever after quit smoking in bed;
And well it would be, for each slave of the weed,
If like the good lady, in time they'd take heed.

WOMAN'S WANTS.

Man wants but little here below;
The gifted poet tells us so;
But woman, I regret to know;
Wants much, all through this vale of woe.

She wants her spouse to keep his place;
And wants her will in every case;
Wants beauty, both in form and face;
And wants admirers of her grace.

She wants a life of perfect ease;
With works of art, and taste to please;
Wants liberty to fret and tease
For every gewgaw that she sees.

She wants no slow old public stage;
But wants a wealth of equipage;
Wants spry young docile handsome page,
And coachman none the worse for age.

Wants other servants by the score;
And wants a mansion running o'er,
From attic to the lowest floor,
With luxuries from every shore.

She wants a full unstinted share,
Of tender, loving, constant care;
Wants jewels, and expensive hair;
Wants laces, furs, and velvets rare.

She wants to have it understood,
Though not achieving all she would;
Her motives ever have been good;
And she has done the best she could.

She wants her rights, with want profound;
And claims that man's in duty bound
To make her ruler, all around;
Leaving no wantage on the ground.

MINE HANS.

Mine Hans, vots my old man you zee.
Him all time try for boss of me.
"Grechen," say he, "why vault you vint,
Man good for rule von voman kint."
Ten ven I shows zum leetle spunk,
Him take a spree and gets tead trunk.
Ven I go pet I locks him out,
Vore mornen he comes loaf about.
Next tay, vile he some stagger valk,
Him blacart tongue pegin to talk.
"Voman," him say, "vot pik tisgrace
You pring py getting out of blace,
Von ting to all the vurlt is blain,
I trink to tround drouble and pain;
I peat you zoundly tat I vill;
Your marriage vow you not vulvill—"
In zelf tefense no time to tink,
I knocks him town quick as a vink;

My goot vire zhovel do the teat,
His vounded face pegin to pleat;
Shust ten I leaf, and leaf for life;
I'll pe no trunken Tuchman's vife;
Soon as tem court gife me a shance
I'll pe tivorced, I'm tun vit Hans.

OLD MAIDS.

Despite all stale and thread-bare jokes,
Old maids are much like other folks;
They often show by far more sense,
Than those who laugh at their expense.

Some of them are, without a doubt,
Worthy as saints we read about;
If others are to faults inclined,
They're like the rest of human kind.

Their great defect, as I am told,
Is growing peevish, prim and old;
Yet let them try their age to hide,
Pert critics snub on every side.

The married dame may scold away,
From early dawn till close of day;
And yet her friends forbearance show,
And say: "Poor dear, she's worried so."

And I have heard her spouse and lord,
'Tis so (I'm standing on my word),
Fret through the day and scold at night,
Then try to prove his conduct right.

But let the ancient maid once slip
One word that patience bids her skip,
It is reported far and near;
She's called eccentric, cross and queer.

Such gossip can have no excuse,
And savors sadly of abuse;
I hate the taunter's ill-bred jokes;
Old maids have hearts like other folks.

A DISAPPOINTED BACHELOR.

With pleasures flown, he lives alone,
  Pent up in reticence;
He bears each joke, unkindly spoke,
  Attempting no defense.

There's no excuse, for the abuse,
  Heaped on his lonely head.
Some woman knows, why he has chose
  The life that he has led.

This may be so, I do not know;
His business is not mine;
Do let him be; why can't you see
That it is none of thine.

For aught you know, long years ago
Death took one from his side;
Who had she stayed, he would have made
His own and cherished bride.

His guarded heart, is loth to part
With secrets all its own.
And it is well, he does not tell
The sorrows he has known.

For few would care, and none would share
The trials of his lot;
His story old, if left untold,
Will sooner be forgot.

MOTHER'S INFLUENCE.

Man is a mother's boy grown tall;
Mostly he's this and that is all;
Describe the mother's traits to me,
I'll tell you what the man will be.

Say not you've seen it otherwise;
Doubtless exceptions will arise;
But, mother's training, good or bad,
Tells on the future of the lad;
And, as a rule, the mother can
Direct the morals of the man.
As twigs are bent, so trees will grow;
Where mothers lead, the children go.

SNOBOCRACY.

Some think this an uncalled-for word;
    Our fathers used it not;
It came to life derisively,
    By latter days begot.
It does not mean democracy,
    In any sense or way;
Nor means it aristocracy;
    Except in false display,
Snobocracy is great pretence,
Combined with much impertinence.

The snob confronteth everywhere;
    Diffusing views unsound;
And sometimes where expected least,
    There doth he most abound.

He is a literary sham;
His dogmas overhauled,
Disclose old errors newly dressed,
Science falsely so called,
Snobocracy is great pretense,
Combined with much impertinence.

"'The fool hath said there is no God;"
The snob says much the same;
And that through evolution, we
From merest atoms came.
By whom those atoms first were made,
He ne'er explains to you;
While he sarcastically declares,
The Bible is untrue.
Snobocracy is great pretence,
Conbined with much impertinence.

Some snobs declaim with eloquence,
Worthy a better cause;
Denying God's omnipotence,
His wisdom and his laws;
The more they talk the more they get
Engulfed in mystic doubt;

Until they prove the fallacy
   Of what they're making out.
Snobocracy is great pretence,
Combined with much impertinence.

GIGGLES AND GAWKS.

What'er you do or leave undone,
Do not forbid a little fun;
Don't rob your boy of childish joy,
Nor grieve your girl with haughty curl
Of your refined sarcastic lip,
Even if she do romp and skip,
Or in some way, while at her play,
Prove she is not the most refined
And ladylike of womankind.
Seem not too harsh or stern in talk.
'Tis natural for boys to gawk;
Should girl or boy gawk, grin and wiggle,
Remember there's a time to giggle.
Keep hopeful; all will yet be right.
Their father took profound delight
In playing with a ball and bat,
And teasing neighbor Fidget's cat;

Their mother, dignified and bland,
In other years, I understand,
While passing through her childhood days,
Had awkward, unbecoming ways;
So be of cheer, and persevere;
With patience, tenderness and love;
Your children may and will improve.

SLAVERY.

WRITTEN 1852.

The pale moon smiled benignly down
On city, hamlet, farm and town;
Soft zephyrs fanned magnolia boughs,
Nature seemed paying God her vows.
Within a hut both rude and old,
There dwelt a man of simple soul;
And near his cot were many more
Like to his own both rude and poor.
Before the hut not far away,
Stood master's house of rich display;
For this poor man of soul so pure,
Was owned by man, and must endure

Whate'er his master pleased to say;
And work, and toil, with naught for pay;
Save what hard-hearted masters give,—
Few clothes, and food enough to live.
At this calm hour he could not sleep,
For o'er his mind this thought would creep,
What if before to-morrow passed,
His wife and child he'd see the last.
For he o'erheard his master say
To-morrow will be auction day,
He wished to have them look their best,
He'd see that they were fitly dressed;
A sickly child would never pay,
They were forever in the way;
And that perhaps it would be best
To sell his boy among the rest.
He did not tell his wife; ah no!
For yet he hoped 'twould not be so,
But his good heart could not forbear
To raise his soul in fervent prayer
That God, who prayer doth ever heed,
Would give him strength in time of need,
'Twas morn at length, that awful morn—
Poor man! he rose with heart forlorn.

This day would tell,—he feared to hear,
Lest he should lose all he held dear.
That day the wife and child were sold.
Yes, human flesh was swopped for gold.
They tore the mother from the child.
Heedless of sobs, frantic and wild.
Full well she knew now they were sold,
Husband or child she'd ne'er behold.
To some plantation far away
She started, for she must obey—
But Oh! her heart was left behind.
Though she was black, she had a mind.
The child soon found a welcome grave,
'Twas better than to be a slave.
The mother ne'er was heard of more;
They'll meet in heaven but not before.
O shameful sin; shame to our States;
A sin God sees, frowns at, and hates.
He knows the sinner and the saint,
And he will hear the slaves' complaint.

LETTER TO AN EDITOR.

Dear Mr. Editor:—

My good old man and I

Were glad to see your "Retrospect," and I will tell
you why:

Because we've read the HERALD these years twenty
three,

And feel as well acquainted with it as we can be.

Twenty-four years ago you see, when I became a
wife,

We picked on the *Evangelist*, and settled down for life.

But before a year was passed, I found my head so
low,

Some weighty truths were shot so high, that over it
they'd go.

I told my husband's father, of wisdom much possessed;

He simply said, the HERALD I think would suit you best.

So then we took the HERALD, and I can understand

The home news as it comes to us, and that from foreign land;

I like to read the Eastern news; of course I do the
West,

I love the Children's Corner," but Pansy's story
best.

I thank you much for "Woman's Work," and "Select
    Paragraph,"
And for your "Wit and Wisdom"—it pleases me to
    laugh.
Of all our periodicals and papers not a few,
We love our old, tried friend the best, the one that
    comes from you.
Please do not think me flattering; I mean each word
    and all,
      Remaining your devoted friend,
             PATTY MARIA SMALL.

USE AND ABUSE.

Two children born across the way,
To be explicit we will say,
Their advent was on New Year's day.

Do not imagine twins were there,
It took two homes to hold the pair,
And each could boast a baby fair.

They seemed as much alike at five,
As two bees quartered in one hive,
Or almost any boys alive.

At ten there'd been a wonderous change,
As thought assumed a wider range,
Each one esteemed the other strange!

One was a Christian, even then,
A lover of his fellow men,
And diligent with book and pen;—

The other was, I grieve to say,
A skeptic, at that early day,
Who, scoffing, said, " Why do they pray?"

At twenty, with their school days o'er,
Each had enough of worldy lore,
For business men, if nothing more.

But, Oh! at this eventful day,
The tempter tried them every way;
And one became an easy prey.

In dissipation's gaudy maze,
The skeptic spent his nights and days,
Nor took he heed unto his ways;

He brought no talent into use,
His health he ruined by abuse,
Then tried to frame a slim excuse.

At thirty, hard; at forty, old,
At fifty, indigent and cold,
His sands of life were almost told.

This life of indolence and blight,
At last went out in endless night,
Without one ray of heavenly light.

The Christian with unceasing prayer,
Was sheltered by Almighty care,
And thus escaped the wily snare.

At thirty, fervent, not obtuse;
His diligence sought no excuse,
But brought each talent into use,

At forty like good men of yore;
"Plenty sat smiling at his door,"
Enough for his and something o'er.

At fifty, he did not seem old,
At sixty, business years were told;
Yet his kind spirit grew not cold.

Revered, beloved by fellow men,
He fell asleep in Jesus, when
He reached his three score years and ten.

This subject is with meaning fraught,
If we receive it as we ought,
There's room for much protracted thought.

ME AND CATARINE.

Zo long as me and Catarine lift in the Fadder land,

None haft zome petter vife tand me, I gift you
   unterstant,

Ant vent ve comes town on tis blace first year she do
   shust right;

She vork outs in te fielt py tay, ant cooks zome voot
   at night;

She mint te house, she milch te cows, make all time
   clean te stable;

She tent te carden, hoes te truck, and vell sees to the
   table.

Zome tay it rain, ant den she vash my shirt all nice
   and cleant;

She zo my pants, and tarn my zocks, zo goot you
   never seent.

Put zoon te vomant on tis lant (I hates dem every one,

Ven I tinks of te mischiefs dem to Catarine haft done.)

Not much dem verk, zo here her come, gossip mine
   house about—

Tell Catarine her vork do much; she's man's a lazy
   lout.

No tebts them say, buildings all fint, and farm zo
   goot and pik.

You ist one voolish vomant now, to vash, scrub,
   scour and dik.

Tehn Catarine her puts on airs, dem larnt her make
zome lace;

Her go vit me in fielt no more—say dat's no vomant's
blace.

Vone tay her take sheself to town, comes home trest
out in zilk;

Her zay "My tear, I no more stout, zo you and Shon
go milch."

My sakes! I mat, ant raise a row; put Catarine she laft,

Zay "Vomans vork in Shermany, put here te man do
haft."

Tehn I zey more loud, vicked vords, till Shon—him
mother's son—

Zay "Tat's enoughs dad, come you on, I milchs te
hardest one."

From dat zame night her milchs no more, but all time
haft her way;

Ant Catarine do boss tist house from tat unhappys
day.

I wish me stay in Fadder-lant; pen tenant all mine
time;

I'd zooner pe one lant-lord's slaft, tand slaft to
Catarine.

LINES TO A FRIEND ON HIS SIXTIETH BIRTHDAY.

Dear, tried old friend, on thy birthday
We meet to cheer thee on thy way;
To thank God for his mercies past,
And hope they may forever last.

We've met thee often—knew thee long—
When each of us were hale and strong;
Have met in joy, likewise in tears,
And now we meet in riper years.

We come in friendly, festive way,
Noting time's milestone—thy birthday;
Feel sure of hearty welcome here,
And honest, frugal, kindly cheer.

We wish thee not great hoarded wealth,
Would rather see thee in good health,
With means each just demand to pay,
And something for a rainy day.

With friends and comfort be thou blest,
'Till thy last days shall be thy best,
And when our earthly meeting's o'er
God grant we meet to part no more.

I MUST, I WILL BE POPULAR.

I must, I will be popular;
   I cannot urge reform;
I cannot bear both sneer and stare,
   I cannot "stem the storm."

I must I will be popular;
   Therefore I leave the right;
My yielding ways will bring me praise,
   And that is my delight.

I must, I will be popular;
   In this progressive day;
Our father's code, their creed and mode,
   Great prejudice display.

I must, I will be popular;
   Though I do clan with vice;
I try to keep conscience asleep,
   Awake its over-nice.

I must I will be popular;
   Regardless of the cost;
Don't trouble me, nor bid me see,
   How much will thus be lost.

SUPERSEDED.

Yes, I am superseded;
  That all can plainly see.
I am no longer needed;
  Earth hath no call for me.
My mate in death is sleeping;
  Our birdling's found a wife.
They two the house are keeping,
  And I've a lonely life.

My bureau's found the garret;
  My bed the little room.
With no one left to share it,
  Oppressive is the gloom.
New carpet, and new curtain;
  New work of strange design
Confronts me, till I'm certain
  This is no home of mine.

They do not treat me badly;
  My grievances are small.
Yet I am wounded sadly,
  And fatal is the fall.
But hush! Am I complaining?
  Nay; let me patient wait
The few brief hours remaining
  This side the "golden gate."

LOVE FROM MY STANDPOINT.

Early impressions leave us not—
First lessons are not soon forgot.
When I was little, long ago,
A dear old grandpa watched me grow.

Patient and brave, he did survive,
Till he was nearly eighty-five;
He was so kind, it seems to me
All good old men beloved should be.

Though quite too sparing of the rod,
My father was a man of God;
By his example, day by day,
He early taught us how to pray.

Faithful he was, to God and man:
A firm believer in the plan
Of man's salvation through our Lord,
As shown us in the sacred word.

My teacher that I loved the best,
Was a professor plainly dressed;
Grave, distant, homely, but refined,
And of a pure and heavenly mind.

My school-day friends did me no harm,
But gave to life a transient charm;
Which, when I tired of, passed away,
And made room for my nuptial day.

Since then my dearest friend in life,
Is he who claims me for his wife;
What wonder that it seems to me,
Men in their prime beloved should be.

Dear baby daughter passed away,
But God allowed my boy to stay;
Obedient, confiding, free,
He proves a constant joy to me.

With boyish sports and laughter gay,
He cheers me through the longest day;
Until it really seems to me,
Such little men beloved should be.

If I should live, feeble and old,
The world without seem drear and cold;
Naomi-like I'll loving be,
If Obed comes to comfort me.

FRANK'S CABBAGE.

Permit me to relate a fact
   That never was in print,
Hoping that some may have the tact
   From it to take a hint.

It transpired near my native place
   A score of years ago,
Before my honored father's face;
   'Twas he that told me so.

Their church seemed at a stagnant stand;
   Was more lukewarm than cold.
No preaching elder led the band;
   The deacons all were old.

Their creed, quite close enough to fit,
   Was safe and nowise dry,
A Baptist wall stood firm on it,
   And rose exceeding high.

Their house of God, built years before,
   Was kept in good repair;
And now they needed something more—
   No parsonage was there.

They prayed and talked and talked and met,
   Yet did but little more,
Until their youths began to fret,
   And wished the talking o'er.

Especially one erring sheep,
   Who often went astray,
By nature not inclined to keep
   The strait and narrow way.

But he had one redeeming trait.
   His business tact was fair;
When passing through financial strait,
   His help was always there.

"Ah, me!" thought Frank, "I've found my
       sphere;
   Here's work in my own line;
We'll have a parsonage this year;
   I'll make the business mine."

A thousand cabbage-heads he raised,
   And sold each for a dime;
And then he said, "The Lord be praised,
   My help will be in time."

Deacon Forbearance loved young Frank,
  Said, "Make your cabbage grow;
I'll bring as much from saving bank
  As you from it can show."

Sister Pricilla Consecrate
  Came forward with her share;
And even Brother Obstinate
  Made contribution fair.

They bought a parsonage that year,
  Just as Frank thought they could,
Without a debt to interfere
  With future plans for good.

The parsonage, in good repair,
  Is doing service still;
And Frank yet lives, not far from there,.
  A man of potent will.

Deacon Forbearance passed away
  A few short years ago;
But during life was heard to say,
  "God made Frank's cabbage grow."

TACT.

It is a melancholy fact
Most people are devoid of tact;
Or else their atom is so small
We really think they've none at all.

It's their misfortune more than sin,
When sharp intriguers take them in.
Fully intending to do right,
They miss it by an oversight.

As long as duty's in a groove
They're willing and know how to move.
But when it calls for change or tact
They simply know not how to act.

Great, cultured people, highly bred,
With stores of knowledge in the head.
Are apt to have an absent mind,
Which with much tact is not combined.

Of all whom we have known or read,
For tact, Paul seems to be ahead.
It's an attainment nowise small,
To be all things and unto all.

But his shrewd mind saw the outcome.
By doing thus he could save some.
We'd have more tact, both you and I,
If we our whims would crucify.

FIRE! FIRE!

Calmly the sabbath morning dawned
    Upon our blithe, sweet home;
Fickle Dame Fortune fondly fawned,
    Saying, thy rest hath come.

We left the dear old home alone,
    For church two miles away,
As we before had often done,
    So did we on this day.

The great, grand maple in the yard
    Fanned out a brief good bye;
No doubt, no fear, the present marred,
    No sense of danger nigh.

I never can forget that ride,
    Nor how our children bright,
While in the carriage side by side,
    Hummed hymns of pure delight.

Bracing and clear the country air,
　　Fragrant the breath of June;
Our God of grace by means thus fair,
　　Set hearts in holy tune.

At church more solemn grew the hour,
　　With sacred songs and prayer,
While Bible lesson's soothing power
　　Dispelled intruding care.

FIRE! FIRE! FIRE!

Dreadful, sudden, astounding sound,
Broke in upon the sweet profound.
Then there was pallor and affright,
And hurried, awkward, trembling flight,
While I, with stupid terror dumb,
Wondered from whence the sound had come.
Without a moments time to waste,
The crier with befitting haste
Shot back as might a frenzied fay,
Toward our loved home two miles away.
Ah! then I saw and had to know,
The rider was our tenant Joe—
Good, faithful servant on the farm,
Meet instrument to sound alarm.

Our house on fire! oh! could it be?
My frightened children clung to me,
How, I weak soul, then tried to pray,
Thy will be done, strove hard to say;
How husband, man like, aimed to show
His strength sufficient for the blow;
How rushed the anxious human tide.
Driver with other driver vied;
How grandly rose the dense black smoke,
Oh! what disaster it bespoke!
But when we saw the bursting blaze,
Excitement grew to frantic craze,
"Till ere we reached the open gate.
The verdict was: Too late! too late!
Wild flames were puffing from the door;
Took upper and the nether floor,
Hissed through the window panes and sash,
The roof fell in with direful crash,
Great red mad sparks went flying 'round,
All things combustible were found—
House, barn, sheds, all, saving the well,
In one great common ruin fell,
Stern desolation hovered 'round,
Charred embers o'er familiar ground;

How did our spirits in us sink,
Think of the anguish—only think!
Gone now my silver, presents, all,
My carpets, pictures on the wall,
My sacred relics of the dead,
Even the lock from Willie's head.

The great grand maple in the yard
   Bowed low its lofty head,
It stood, but stood defaced and scarred,
   Scorched, shriveled up and dead.

That night, all weary, sick and faint,
   A neighbor took us in;
I could not utter harsh complaint,
   And I had sadder been.

Far sadder was my mother heart
   A year before: the day
When we with Willie had to part—
   God took our child away.

I felt that all with him was well,
   His soul to God was given,
Yet it seemed hard on earth to dwell,
   With Willie gone to heaven.

Two busy years have flitted fast,
  And we've another home,
But precious Willie of the past,
  Can never to us come.

Yet we shall shortly to him go,
  Like David to his child;
The blessed book doth tell me so,
  And I am reconciled.

THE POOR MAN'S HOUR.

In the early gray of morning,
  Ere sun displays its power;
When the city's hosts are sleeping,
  The poor man has his hour.

He comes from tidy cottage,
  From crowded rooms and court,
And from neglected alley
  Where idle children sport.

Comes with firm step and cheerful,
  To honest labor now;
No doubt his bread is sweeter
  Forsweating of the brow.

He comes with self-denial,
  To toil for home and love;
His God approves his effort
  And aids him from above.

He comes, with hopes undaunted,
  With naught to make afraid;
A poor but useful host are they—
  The brave bucket brigade.

The giddy-gaudy fashon bird,
  At this hour of the day,
Draws no admirers, makes no calls,
  But dreameth time away.

The victim of midnight debauch,
  And he who raised the row,
Though brawling on the street last night,
  Are somewhere else just now.

The poor man's unmolested,
  He seems to reign alone;
The busy, bustling world's asleep;
  This hour is all his own.

When many come from north and south,
  And sit down with the blest—
God grant the poor man then may have
  An endless hour of rest.

ODE TO VERMONT.

Grand old Vermont of rocky hills,
Of healing springs and romping rills.
Of mountains capped with snow so bright,
'Bove hills of evergreen and white.

Your health-diffusing mountain air
Comes puffing o'er the valley fair,
Gayly disturbs the quiet lake,
And calls on languid life to wake.

The shrieking train comes curving round
To reach a cool, secluded town,
When lo! what piles of marble white
Astound the beauty-loving sight.

Vermont, so staunch in Church and State,
No wonder that your sons are great;
Your fair, learned women are no toys.
But peers of your "Green Mountain Boys."

Your statesmen, sculptors and your clerks,
Poets, dairies and sugar-works,
Are strangely blended, and should be
Where all are cultured, brave and free.

Your noisy, booming river falls,
Your winter storms and summer squalls,
Played anthems in my childhood's ear
Such as I'm longing now to hear.

Each village has a spacious green,
And streets both wide and long and clean;
But, oh, that cottage on the hill,
I'm weeping—for I see it still.

Vermont, so weird, so quaint, so old,
Your country charms can ne'er be told;
Vermont, Vermont, no pen can tell
How much I love you, and how well.

* ⬥ *

BETTY LOVED HER DUNCAN.

[AN INCIDENT OF THE WAR OF 1812.]

Poor Betty was a winsome lass, a bonnie Scottish
    dame;
She never bothered much with books, nor hankered
    after fame.

She kept her cottage tidied up and Duncan's linen
white,

And had his supper nice and warm when he came
home at night.

For Betty loved her Duncan and had loved him all
her life,

So Duncan was a happy man when she became his wife.

He was a sailor father's son, this stalwart highland
brave ;

The father, ere he saw his son was buried 'neath the
wave.

His mother lived to press her babe once fondly to
her breast,

Then meekly closed her eyes on earth, and entered
into rest.

His stricken grandam nursed him then, and fed him
from a cup,

And tended to his many wants until she brought him up;

And when he wed with Betty she fairly wept for joy,

And cried God bless his bonnie bride and my brave
soldier boy.

For Betty loved her Duncan and had loved him all
her life,

So proudly gave her hand to him, when she became
his wife.

Two happy years of wedded life with them passed
    swift away,

Then grandma's waiting spirit flew to realms of end-
    less day.

'Twas well for her that then she went, for had she
    lingered more,

She'd seen their Duncan leave his home to fight on
    foreign shore.

When Betty found that he must go, she nothing did
    but weep.

Her cottage was neglected quite, and neither could
    she sleep,

Her wee bairn, Sandy, who had been her comfort,
    pride and care,

She now pressed wildly to her breast, in agony and
    prayer,

But there was little time for tears, the fleet sailed
    boldly out.

And brave hearts covered up their fears, and stifled
    back their doubt.

Sandy slept soundly through it all on Betty's mother's
    bed,

And when she came not soon to him, she wept alone,
    they said;

But when they called and searched for her and she
could not be found,

They thought that she had frantic grown and her
poor self had drowned.

For Betty loved her Duncan, and had loved him all
her life,

So could not bear to part with him, poor Betty, Duncan's wife.

Long days, and weeks, and months rolled on, at last
a letter came;

Saying that Betty hoped her friends would think her
not to blame,

For they could never, never know, the sorrow of her
heart;

Nor half the struggle that it cost her, with them all
to part,

The last night Duncan stood on guard, he slipped
her on the boat;

And 'mong the freight secreted her, until they were
afloat.

When fairly out at sea she stood up, trembling, by
his side;

He never knew which most he felt, a sense of fear
or pride.

None, high or low spoke harsh to her, not one e'en
    grew too bold;
But rough, brave men respected her and thought her
    noble souled.
For Betty loved her Duncan, and had loved him all
    her life.
So left her friends and child for him; brave Betty,
    Duncan's wife.
Stormy and long, their voyage proved, across the
    briny wave,
Many grew weary, longed for home, some found an
    ocean grave.
But when they reached the western world and soldiers
    marched on shore,
Poor Betty felt a loneliness, she never felt before.
An officer of rank who saw her young and saddened
    face,
Showed kindly interest in them, and soon found her
    a place;
In worthy Christian family she worked a long sad year,
Before the cruel war was o'er and Duncan could
    appear
To claim his faithful, loving wife, and place her in a cot,
Among the grand Green Mountain hills, a cool and
    quiet spot.

They seemed so much like Scottish hills, she loved
>   her new found home,
And only wished, and hoped, and prayed, their boy
>   might to them come.
'Twas all in vain, they never saw his face again on
>   earth,
Although he lived to comfort her, who gave his
>   mother birth.
And Betty lived, and Duncan too, their three-score
>   years or more,
And children, and grandchildren, played around
>   their humble door.
In ripe old age her Duncan left his Betty here below,
And then she learned how much of grief her poor
>   old heart could know.
For over forty years she clung in fondness to his side;
The saddest day of Betty's life was when her Dun-
>   can died.
But God was very merciful, she had not long to wait
Before he took her o'er the stream, and through the
>   heavenly gate.
For Betty loved her Duncan, and had loved him all
>   her life.
So died in hope of meeting him; blest Betty, Dun-
>   can's wife.

WHY THIS MOURNING?

WRITTEN ON THE DEATH OF PRESIDENT GARFIELD.

We waited for tidings, and sad tidings came,
Though nursing was perfect, no surgeon to blame;
Though prayer was incessant, his great spirit fled;
Our God approved ruler now rests with the dead.

The son of the widow is borne to the grave,
The Christian died trusting the Mighty to save;
The husband and father domestic'ly blest,
Relinquished earth's treasures, for Heavenly rest.

The soldier fell not in the battle's mad strife,
The rider on horseback escaped with his life,
One lone weak assassin, with villainous hand,
Sends no common mourning through our beloved land.

Why had we such trouble, such trembling, such doubt?
Why was he left mangled to ebb his life out?
Why did God permit it, why did our chief die?
Our spirits lamenting repeat the sad why?

God saw our pretentions, our vain love of show,
Saw sin in high places, pollution in low,
Saw party dissension stalk forth at midday,
Politic ambition determined to sway.

So there came the mourning, as it came once before,
When war clouds were lifted, and battles were o'er;
When our noble leader, whose heart swelled with love,
Was called from his labors, to mansions above.

God sent these afflictions, in mercy we trust,
He saw our souls needed an humbling to dust;
And that our sins called for bereavement and care,
Before we could offer acceptable prayer.

HOLIDAY ACROSTICS.

I

Feeble, compared with the mighty of earth,
Our nation appeared at the time of its birth,
Union developed the strength we possessed,
Righteous the true God on whose arm we rest.
Through trials and troubles hath he been just,
Holy, omnipotent; in him we trust.

On this birthday of our beloved nation,
Faith looks aloft to the God of salvation.

Justice and mercy in him do combine,
United graces continue to shine,
Language can never his glory express,
Yet he is ready and willing to bless.

II

Trustingly, thankfully, let us rejoice;
Honestly, heartily, lift up the voice,
All over the nation, here and elsewhere;
Nature is calling for praises and prayer.
Kindly God filleth our basket and store;
So let us thank him, as never before,
Gifts of the spirit, far more precious still,
In great abundance, we have if we will,
Vain, inconsistent, and transient are we,
In him immortal perfection we see,
Now let devotion, and faith have the sway,
Giving God glory on Thanksgiving Day.

III

Merry Christmas; Let it ring;
Earth and air unite, and bring
Royal honors to our King;
Ransomed saints to Jesus cling;
Yea, "Peace, good will," th' angels sing!

Christ is here—the living Head;
Hope, ye souls who once were dead!
Ruler, prophet, priest was he;
Innocent he died, that we

Sinners, sick and sunk in woe,
To a healing fount might go,
Mercy peace and pardon know,
All who trust him and believe,
Shall eternal life receive.

IV

Happy New Year; truly we
All have cause to happy be;
Peace and plenty smile around,
Perfect pardon may be found;
Yea, free grace doth yet abound.

Now the dear old year hath fled,
Entered rest with noiseless tread;
Wrong they are who call it dead.

Years and times are in God's hand;
Each in proper order stand;
Ages past have found him just;
Resting on his word, we trust.

UNCLE JABEZ.

Grave, stern, uncle Jabez was grandmother's brother
The only known relative left to our mother.
He lived in the mansion on Hyacinth Hill;
We, in a snug cottage near Peppermint Rill.

The world thought him gifted, and sought his advice;
But he sought not, found not, the pearl of great price;
So while with earth's bounties his coffers ran o'er,
His soul was neglected, his heart, sick and sore.
Uncle Jabez took harshly the sorrows of life,
Became almost frantic at losing his wife;
And when called to part with his sister and child,
Grew fiercely rebellious and unreconciled.
He did not, he could not, wholly neglect;
The ward his dead sister left him to protect.
Yet, his august presence, his bearing severe;
The shy little orphan eluded with fear.
But Prudence, the house-wife, was thoughtful and good;
And Betty, his cook, did the best that she could.
Miss Primrose, her teacher, wise patient and nice,
Gave wholesome instruction and heeded advice.
With them grew our mother like plant in the shade,
A fragile, pale blossom, a delicate maid.
Not even suspecting the hidden affection,
Transferred from the dead, by a man's recollection.
Yet uncle did love and protect in his way;
Though seldom, so seldom, had he aught to say,
That the child o'er his grounds, through his house a
          free ranger;
Grew up by his side, a comparative stranger.

Old scenes were reacted, we mortals will mate,
Uncle Jabez's resentment amounted to hate.
He part with his Agnes, his sister Ruth's child?
The thought was preposterous, wicked and wild!
What had the young suitor to offer a wife?
No home, and no comforts, no prospects in life.
They need not be waiting on him for consent,
She could marry in haste, at her leisure, repent.

* * * * * * * * * * * * *

There was love in the cottage near Peppermint Rill,
While dreary discomfort took Hyacinth Hill.
Uncle Jabez, grown miserly, feeble and cross,
Kept ever lamenting his sorrow and loss.
Six children were given our parents in all,
But dear little Mary was taken when small
To the bright home in glory, the land of the blest,
Where Christ and his angels watch over her rest.
In this uncle Jabez saw no cause for grief,
Believed that her absence would prove a relief,
One less back to cover, one less mouth to feed,
One less girl to rush into trouble and need.
We were poor, with poverty past all denying,
A poverty pinching. pervading and trying;

But never in all these years of tough training
Did mother repine or decend to complaining.
Sometimes when his business called father away,
Would uncle come to us, and sit by the day;
While dear mother, cheerful, despite of her care,
Extended him welcome and sympathy there.
The mansion from dreary to dreadful had grown,
A hermit, a miser, dwelt there all alone;
Sometimes a man-servant was hacking about,
But women, save mother, were ever shut out.
When sick, she would nurse him for weeks at a time,
Yet never was tendered thanks, dollar or dime.
" Poor Agnes," he'd say, "you might have been rich,
Instead of low down there in poverty's ditch.
And I could live nicer were it not for you—
You'll need all my hoardings before you are through.
But then—women must and will have their way,
And you have had your's I am happy to say."
But change marketh all things on this transient earth.
And change came at last to the desolate hearth.
Uncle Jabez lay moaning at death's yawning door.
More wretched and helpless, than ever before.
He wailed like an infant, were she out of sight,
So mother stayed by him through day and through
    night,

Unfailing and tender, in daughterly care,
Prevailing, unceasing, yet secret, in prayer.
She prayed his rebellion and warfare might cease,
Repentance be followed by pardon and peace,
And God heard his hand-maid, regarded her care,
And answered, yea, far more than answered her
    prayer.
Almost imperceptibly, came there a change.
Convalescent, much better, recovered! How strange!
Yet stranger to us, seemed the calmness and rest
Possessing the hitherto turbulent breast.
He said, "I will fight my convictions no more,
I trust that my bondage to Satan is o'er,
And Agnes, this must be the heavenly birth,
This comfort surpassing emotions of earth.
I know I am weak, but my Savior is strong;
Oh, why did I slight, and reject him so long!
Yet I've a presentiment of peaceful old age,
In some humble service I yet may engage."
And uncle did live, ten full years and more.
He could not atone for life wasted before.
But his walk was consistant, his peace like a river;
His gratitude constant to God, the great giver.
He hovering around with a fatherly care,
Gave mother the means for all needed repair,

Then, firmly declaring the cottage too small,
Insisted the mansion should shelter us all.
To this father gave a reluctant consent;
Concession he ne'er had a cause to repent.
For the new home of comfort was tranquil and fair,
And mother, dear mother, sole mistress and heir.
Though now uncle Jabez is with us no more,
We feel that he only has gone on before.
For he went with assurance his sins were forgiven,
And for him was waiting a mansion in heaven.

THE SAILOR'S STORY.

Time had dealt kindly with me as any man alive;
When I attained my best estate at nearing thirty-five.
I'd been a jolly sailor, for fifteen solid years;
Had learned to laugh at land-men's whims, and wond-
    er at their fears.
Yet I was born and bred upon an old Kentucky farm;
And memories of my early years had never lost their
    charm.
I went to sea because it seemed the thing for me to do,
Since Captain Humes, good uncle John, was anxious
    for me to.

A Christian in the strictest sense, was sterling uncle
  John;
While sailing o'er life's stormy seas his spirit's bark
  sped on
Straight toward the port of perfect peace, the harbor
  where the just,
Who live by faith, shall rest for aye in haven of their
  trust.
His creed was purely what he learned while at his
  mother's knee;
In all its grand simplicity, he taught it o'er to me.
And all his crew, without exempt, were led to under-
  stand
That God was God, upon the sea, as on the solid land.
When bowed by age, he worried not; but to his cabin
  took,
A faithful, patient, waiting saint, contented with the
  Book.
I knew he meant to die at sea, was willing that he
  should,
Since he was happiest where he was, and deemed my
  nursing good.
Little by little he resigned his cares into my hand,
Till months before he passed away I had the full
  command.

Calmly he died, and sea life then for me lost all its
    charm;

I longed to see my friends and home, longed for the
    good old farm.

Longed most for one who ne'er had been far from my
    busy mind,

The playmate of my early youth; the girl I left behind.

Although her mother thought not best that we should
    correspond,

Still, in my secret heart of hearts, I cherished Nellie
    Bond.

Mother was gone before I left; in one year father died;

And, ere another year rolled round, sister became a
    bride.

Brother, who kept the dear old home, wrote kindly
    oft and long,

Reminding me of boyish hopes, love, laughter, sports
    and song.

Freely he spoke of married life, and begged me
    understand

His household longed to welcome me when'er I came
    to land.

But never once wrote he a word of little Nellie Bond;

I do suppose that he forgot I once of her was fond.

Some hours had been monotonous; but, always hale
and strong,
I'd lightly noted days and years, as they had passed
along.
Much had I seen, and read, and hoped; but little had
I thought
What changes in my native place, these fifteen years
had wrought.
Unlike most men who go to sea, I never cared to roam;
My uncle's heir I now had means for comforts, and a
home.
So, dreaming of domestic bliss, I sought my native
shore
Expecting I should be content to never leave it more.
A puffing, shrieking, smoking, train dashed through
the little town,
Halting just long enough to set me and my baggage
down.
Change! change! were these the very streets I trav-
ersed when a boy?
Strange, sad, foreboding, anxious thoughts now min-
gled with my joy.
"Home from a foreign land," they sing,—was thi
dull place my home?

How shrank and lonely seemed the church! how
    pitiful the dome!

I hastened to my parent's graves; the dead no tales
    can tell,

But lives had told me years before that all with them
    was well.

But hark! the puny church bell tolled a feeble, plain-
    tive din,

A few plain dames in clean attire came walking slow-
    ly in.

" Poor thing," said one, who spoke too loud, " she's
    done with pain at last,

I'm glad for her dear patient sake that all is o'er and
    past.

Ten years ago, who would have thought he'd filled a
    drunkard's grave,

And she would lie in death to-day more lowly than a
    slave ?"

I followed with the few who came to lay away the
    dead.

Something was said of last sad rites, then this was
    slowly read,—

Mary Ellen Bond Badette was born, married and died;

On such and such and such a time, What else was
    read beside

I never knew,—this was too much; my poor heart
    whirlpooled round
From love's high, fond expectancy to sorrow's sad
    profound.
A sickening, surging, saddening wail went sweelling
    through the room,
It roused me from my reverie and shocked me in my
    gloom.
Three little shrinking, frightened waifs wept 'round
    the coffin's head
"Wake, mamma, wake! dear mamma, wake!" they
    o'er and over said.
Who lay in that rude coffin there? had I come home
    for this?
Where, all my hopes of love returned, my dreams of
    wedded bliss?
Where, charms matured, beauty and trust, that I had
    thought to find?
Where, cultured lady, waiting me, with undivided
    mind?
No semblance of the maid I left, was in that haggard
    face;
Only a drunkard's widow dead, crushed 'neath her
    great disgrace.

One thing reminded of the past, one thing and nothing more,—

On that poor corpse I saw a ring that I had seen
before.

My heart, with one great struggling throe, buried its
love and strife;

Though her pure soul was past reproach, she'd been
another's wife.

Composed I walked from that lone grave, nothing of
mine was there,

Nor were those children more to me than any orphans
are.

A firm brisk step came up behind, a strong arm clasped
my back,

A merry, manly voice rang out, "You're welcome,
brother Jack!"

Father, though dead, still on me smilled in fond,
paternal pride;

Or was it brother, older grown, that stood there by
my side?

Ah, then how much we had to say of now and long
ago!

Each told the other of his weal, but nothing of his
woe.

The dear, old home had much improved; brother had
worked and planned,

And though Kentucky felt the war, plenty still filled
his hand.

For twenty years his wife had proved a solace and
delight,

His girls were fair, his boys were strong, and all were
good and bright.

Sister was sister, sweet and kind as in her childhood's
day,

Though she'd a husband and a son, and was a trifle
gray.

Fifteen more fleeting years have passed, I've comforts,
home and wife

And precious children of my own, who hourly cheer
my life.

I love the boundless briny sea, it came from God's
own hand;

But, blest with these domestic ties, I'm anchored to
the land.

PATIENT REAR-WORKERS.

The daring worker in the van
Is lauded by his fellow-man,
But who was ever heard to cheer
The patient toiler in the rear?

"Honor to whom honor is due."
We would not rob the honored few
Who go before in work or plan,
That bettereth the lot of man.

But then, the lengthy rank and file,
Lowly, but faithful all the while,
Must, when the laureled front may rest,
Plod on unnoticed and unblest.

But God, who doeth all things well,
Can every thought and motive tell.
He, when the victor hath the spoil,
Doth well reward these sons of toil.

BREVITIES.

PURITANICAL.

They call me Puritanical,
Too strict for now-a-days,
And think I ought to fall in rank
With their new fangled ways.
They say I am beside myself,
Though neither learned nor mad,—
Say 'tis the Puritanic taint
That I have always had.

STYLES.

The most of rhymes are only trash,
That with our finer feelings clash,
Still, poetry I do suppose,
May be more elegant than prose;
Yet, I do not pretend to know;
My comprehension is so low,
That poetry and fiction high,
I do not understand nor try.
There's substance in plain English prose,
That speaks of only what it knows;
And don't attempt to soar so high,
To flat out sudden by and by.

EXTREMES.

I can conceive of naught so low,
As woman in her meanest woe.
Save God, I think of naught more great,
Than woman in her best estate.
Without a doubt one demon can
Take full possession of a man.
But woman, though possessed of seven,
Becomes a saint and enters heaven.

A POET.

A poet thinks a poet's mind
Is something wonderf'ly refined;
But other people, of much sense,
See through the bombast and pretence;
And find, when all is boiled down,
But little past the common clown.

RECEIPT FOR PUMPKIN PIE.

Select a pumpkin ripe and nice,
Remove the seeds, scrape, peel and slice.
Stew five hours in an iron pot,
O'er steady fire, not very hot,

Stir often as it simmers down,
Till it is thick, well done and brown,
Then take it up, and let it stand;
Till you can mash it with your hand;
A spoon thrice heaped both good and high
Is quite enough to make a pie,
A cup of good rich milk then add,
One well beat egg, or 'twill be sad;
A spoon twice filled with sugar'll do,
A little salt, and ginger too;
Then bake it with an under crust,
Have good quick fire, indeed you must,
For let it poach, and slowly dry,
You spoil the best of pumpkin pie,
But if you do just as I say,
And bake it on thanksgiving day,
It will be good enough for me,
Yourself, or any *Kumpanee.*

TO MRS. ————— ——

I knew thee not in childhood's day,
Nor yet when it had passed away
And thou wast in thy girlhood's prime,—
That sunny, misty, reign-beau time,

When we first met, you'd learned to know
That life was real,and really so;
And that your part to act in life
Was that of woman, teacher, wife.

* * * * * * * * *

I will not wish thee free from care,
For every mortal has his share.
'Tis vain to wish the free from woe,
For all must share it here below.

But I do hope and trust you may
Have grace sufficient for your day,
And, when the toils of life are o'er,
You'll rest in peace forevermore.

FIND THY BROTHER.

Hast thou found the blessed Savior?
   Is he precious to thy heart?
The world notes thy behavior—
   Go, the glad news impart.
But ere you seek another,
   Search thine own house around—
Remember his own brother
   Was the first that Andrew found.

FIRST HOMES.

First sweet home of childhood's years
Oft I think of thee with tears;—
First sweet home of wedded love
Next to that blest home above,—
If earth's first homes great transports see
What must heaven's first enraptures be?

HEAVEN.

To dwell forever in God's sight,
From doubts and fears set free,
My every thought and feeling right
Is heaven enough for me.

INDEX TO FIRST LINES.

www.ingramcontent.com/pod-product-compliance
Lightning Source LLC
Chambersburg PA
CBHW020612030726

47497CB00007B/2202